Furever Enchanted

A Magical Realism Novel

B. E. Bang

Belle Ink Books

BELLE INK BOOKS

An Imprint of Belle Ink Publishers LLC, Denver

First published in the United States of America by Belle Ink Books, an imprint of Belle Ink Publisher

Visit us online at BelleInkPublishers.com.

Library of Congress Cataloging-in-Publication Data is available.

ISBN 979-8-9913455-3-8 (Paperback)

ISBN 979-8-9913455-8-3 (E-Book)

Cover Illustration Alexandra Zaytseva

Cover Illustration © 2024, Belle Ink Books

Developmental Editing by Ravenn Bang

Copy and Line Editing by Sasha Bent

Proofreading by Sasha Bent

Formatting by Belle Ink Books

Acknowledgements

This book never would have happened without one special Chow having come into my life in April 2017. I owe so much to you Baby Bear. I know I wasn't a perfect pet parent, but I hope you know that I loved you. Still love you. I hope you are either resting in peace on the other side or have moved on to a better life. This book never would have happened without you.

Special thanks to my twin Ravenn for supporting my dream of publishing a book and listening to me talk about the ins-and-outs of making this book a reality. I appreciate you taking the time to read my first draft and this book wouldn't be nearly as much fun without your feedback.

Thanks to my friends, Gracie, Katie, Erzhena, Eunice, Angie, Amanda, Judy, and many others who also supported my author dreams (and sometimes delusions).

Thank you Mom, for frequently taking us to the library as kids and letting us max out the card every single time.

Author's Note

I started writing this book after trying for a year to write a memoir about the time I had with my Chow Chow, Baby Bear. I adopted her on April 21, 2017 when she was estimated to be around seven years old. I lost her on October 29, 2022. Arthritis. She started pain management at eight with Carprofen and Gabapentin. Eventually we added on Adequan shots I gave her at home. At some point, everything just stopped working. I was devastated.

After failing to write a memoir, due to the guilt and regrets that always accompany grief, I decided to try fiction instead. After watching movies like *Everything Everywhere All At Once* (2022) and *Polite Society* (2023), I got the idea to take a mundane situation and make it extraordinary.

This book is not the next great American novel. It probably could have been better if I'd given myself a longer timeline, but I challenged myself to get it done and sometimes things don't have to be perfect. It's just a fun story. Set your expectations accordingly and enjoy.

Peace and Love,

B. E. Bang

P.S. If you haven't seen *Polite Society* (2023), it's so fun. You should watch it.

Chapter 1

Monday

Red and blue lights flashed as Zuri turned onto her street. Thankfully, not in front of her place, but they were close. Too close.

After pulling into her driveway and turning off the engine, she stepped out of her car and looked across the narrow side road at Mr. and Mrs. Lopez's house. With the police cars parallel parked on the curb, she didn't have a clear view of what was going on, but their window was definitely smashed.

"It's just terrible," Donna, Zuri's next-door neighbor, commented from her driveway.

They shared a single wall, Zuri's bedroom and Donna's garage. Donna was a good and mostly quiet neighbor, but also a nosy one. The woman constantly looked out her window and often stopped Zuri to chat if she caught her coming or going.

"Another break-in?" Zuri slid her laptop bag over her shoulder and slammed her car door shut, stepping closer to Donna. Donna turned her walker to face Zuri.

"Yeah, only this time someone was home. I saw an ambulance take Mr. Lopez."

She hoped Mr. Lopez would be okay, but the man was in his early seventies. Not exactly prime recovery age.

"It's the third break-in this month. You'd think they'd have caught them by now. Clearly someone is watching the neighborhood. It could even be somebody who lives here." Donna huffed, annoyed by the incompetence of the officers.

Zuri glanced around at the small community of single-story stucco condos. It was only about fifty units, give or take. Three houses broken into in less than a month. That wasn't random. They were being targeted.

Although it wasn't a fifty-five and up community, most of the houses were owned by older couples and empty nesters. Each condo had a decent size of 1,200 square feet, making them ideal for downsizing from larger family homes. At thirty-one, Zuri was an anomaly. She'd bought her unit a couple of years ago and mostly kept to herself, except when it came to Donna, who didn't give her much of a choice.

Every unit had their own little yard, and everyone had a garage or carport. Nearly all the front yards were subject to xeriscaping with drought and heat-resistant plants or just boring rocks because the intense Arizona spring, summer, and fall temperatures killed most plants. The HOA insisted on keeping grass around their small pool area just to the left, across from Zuri's unit, but it proved more difficult to keep it green every year. The neighborhood was nothing fancy to look at. It was fairly average, and before the recent break-ins, things had always been quiet.

"Isn't your family worried about you living here all by yourself?" Donna asked, actual concern in her eyes.

"My family and I aren't close. So no, I doubt they'd be worried about this at all."

It was true. While she was no orphan, she was still more or less on her own in the world.

The child support paid to her mother was the only evidence she had a father for most of her childhood. Her parents split up before she finished elementary school and once her father moved out, she hadn't seen or heard from him again. No birthday cards. No graduation gifts. Just gone. Zuri didn't miss him or pine for the missing father figure in her life.

Her mother was another story. They had been close once, or she thought they had. But that was before expanding her world in college. Before realizing that something was wrong. Before therapy. A lot of therapy.

Zuri hadn't spoken to her mom much in the last few years apart from a quick phone call every now and then. Usually, if her mom called, she needed something. Sometimes just an ear to vent to, like six months ago, when her last boyfriend had suddenly ended things. Mostly money. It wasn't the typical mother-daughter relationship, but it was all she knew. She stopped hoping for anything different a long time ago.

"Consider getting a roommate, or even better, a husband," Donna said, drawing Zuri out of her thoughts.

"What?" Zuri shook her head. "No, I like living alone."

Images of the many different places she'd lived growing up flashed through her mind. None of them truly hers. The apartments and houses of her mother's boyfriends. Her grandparents' house. Temporary student housing. Never a space that belonged to her the way her house did now, and always spaces occupied with the presence and energy of other people.

She couldn't imagine giving up the sanctity of her home to a roommate, and if she sought a spouse (which she wouldn't), it would be a wife, not a husband. Zuri didn't bother telling Donna that. No need to delve into specifics with her. Not that she thought Donna was homophobic or anything.

She just had an aversion to divulging too much information. She liked to keep to herself. It was easier that way.

"Get a dog then. No one should be completely alone." Donna then shuffled inside her unit without giving Zuri a second glance, probably to cook a feast for her husband and the son and grandchildren living with her.

She looked at the scene across the street one last time, then headed inside as well. She kicked off her shoes and gently placed her laptop bag onto her oversized mustard couch before striding over to the kitchen to make some tea.

Her home was clean and cozy. Everything had a place. Houseplants covered corner shelves or hung on macrame planters near windows. Tall, dark bookshelves covered a single wall from floor to ceiling in both her bedroom and living room. The shelves were all filled to the brim with books she'd either read or wanted to read, mostly the latter.

Every time Zuri looked at the shelves, she felt a sense of calm wash over her. Her mother had never let her buy books growing up. With how often they moved, she always had to consider box weight. Then there was money. They were always short on cash. Now that she was grown, had her own place and her own money, she could buy as many books as she liked. Especially since she didn't plan to move anytime soon.

After pouring water from her filtered water pitcher into her electric kettle to boil, she opened the white kitchen cabinet and took out her favorite blue mug. She grabbed her glass tea infuser from the counter and added some turmeric chai loose leaf tea, also her favorite, before pouring in the hot water.

No matter how hot it was outside, nothing beat the aroma of her spicy herbal tea, paired with a warm blanket on the couch.

Leaving her tea to steep, she walked to the bathroom, grabbed a hair tie, and pulled her dark, curly hair into a high ponytail. The feeling of her hair being pulled back was comforting. Lately, she tried wearing it down more often, as others responded better to her that way. Well, white people did. The only other black woman working at her company was older than Zuri and always telling her she should "do something" with her hair (aka straighten it). Despite few wins with her hair, she intended to maintain its current state: how God made it.

Mixed, half-white and half-black, Zuri had soft curly hair that defied gravity. She vaguely remembered sitting in the living room in front of her father while he wrestled with it in the morning before school and she tried to focus on the cartoons instead of her tender scalp. After he left, she had to fend for herself.

She used to straighten it, because her mom liked it that way, but somewhere around college, she decided to stop appealing to Eurocentric beauty standards and go natural. It drove a wedge between her and her mother, who had nothing nice to say about her hair after that.

After washing her face and hands, she poured her tea, grabbed her tablet, and got under her blanket on the couch, ready to read a few chapters of her latest sci-fi book she started the night before. It was a short novella series by Martha Wells about a remarkably relatable android who referred to themselves as Murderbot. It was amazing.

Despite her efforts to concentrate on her book, she couldn't escape the glimpses of red and blue police lights that peeked through the living room curtains. Donna's suggestions continued to circle in her head.

A roommate was out of the question. All three of her college roommates had been complete slobs. Clothing strewn about and old leftovers littering the fridge. Dishes left unwashed in the sink for days. There had even been one unfortunate incident where she'd walked in on her roommate with a tinder date nakedly entangled on the living room sofa. She had never been able to sit on that couch again.

She could buy cameras or one of those video doorbells to deter the thieves, but she didn't like the idea of her home constantly being monitored. There were plenty of videos online about hackers watching people and even talking to them through their cameras. The thought alone made her shudder.

She would be fine. No need for cameras or a roommate. Everything would be fine.

For some reason, it was always when her head hit her pillow that her brain decided everything would not be fine.

Zuri tossed and turned. It was late. Really late. She wasn't exactly an early bird, more of a night owl than anything else, but 2:30 a.m. was well past her usual bedtime. She needed to get some rest, if only she could fall asleep.

Creak

She sat up and swung her legs over the side of the bed. Sighing, she checked the kitchen, living room, and office for signs of intrusion for the 100th time. There was nothing and no one. Just another normal house noise. Or a ghost. Either was preferable to an intruder. After peeing for the 99th time, she climbed back into bed.

Donna might have been right. If she couldn't stand having a roommate or security cameras, maybe she should get a dog. Dogs didn't bark at normal house noises. Okay, sometimes they did, but she wouldn't get an anxious dog. The house couldn't handle more anxiety. Not with her around.

Zuri liked dogs. She always thought she would get one someday, but she kept finding reasons to wait. At first it was the money. Pets were expensive. Then it was a trip planned. A busy work schedule. The list kept growing, and it never felt like the right time. Now could be the best opportunity she had.

But could she keep a dog alive? She had plants. Most of them had survived at least a year, which was basically forever in houseplant time. She could do this.

She grabbed her phone off the nightstand and found the nearest animal shelter.

Tails Animal Shelter: We choose the right furever friend for you.

The shelter wasn't far, just a few miles down the street. She looked through their newly adoptable dogs. Tons of Pit Bulls and a few Lab mixes. She wanted, no, needed a big dog, to ward off potential thieves, but preferred something fluffier.

She scrolled a little longer until she found a Husky named Max. The large dog sported a fluffy gray and white coat. His eyes called out to her, begging her to break him out of the cage-like kennel. If you looked up "puppy eyes" in a dictionary, Max's face would be the picture under the definition.

This was it. She'd go to the shelter when they opened and rescue Max. Starting tomorrow, she'd be a dog mom.

Her brain started spinning with all the things she needed. Dog food. A leash. Dog beds. Bowls. Treats. Poop bags. Instead of falling asleep, she spent the next hour reading about Huskies on her phone and making a list of everything she needed to buy. Tomorrow promised to be a long, busy day.

Chapter 2

Tuesday

Zuri pulled up to the shelter at exactly 10 a.m. Her car was the only one in the visitor parking lot, probably because it was a Tuesday morning. She called out from work after her mostly sleepless night. Her schedule was flexible and nothing she did was an emergency. She was ahead in her work on the team's current project, so she could afford an unexpected day off. Anyway, paid time off was meant to be used.

It wasn't until around 4 a.m. that she had finally fallen asleep. Unfortunately, her alarm started blaring at 8:30 a.m. Too anxious that her dream dog would be gone if she didn't get to the shelter when they opened, Zuri quickly washed her face, changed, and was out of the house in no time.

First on the list was to buy pet supplies. She couldn't bring a dog home with no supplies. That would be irresponsible. Now her trunk was completely full.

At the pet shop closest to the shelter, she bought three extra-large memory foam dog beds. One to match the aesthetic of her bedroom, office, and living room. One might have been enough, but she wanted to make sure the dog would be comfortable in each of the rooms she spent a lot of time in.

A large bag of dry dog food and a small case of canned wet food, for variety, took up a good chunk of space. She hoped it was good quality, considering the price.

Taking up considerably less space in her trunk was a purple leash and matching white ceramic food and water bowls that would suit her white and green kitchen. Treats and chews recommended by the store associate filled at least two grocery bags. After adding in several toys, she had already dropped at least five hundred dollars on a dog she hadn't even adopted yet.

She watched as a shelter employee unlocked the front doors while she took a sip of her venti flat white. The rich, bold taste helped calm her nerves. It was hard to tell if she was more anxious about adopting a dog, or her house potentially being robbed.

Now or never.

Zuri hopped out of her car and walked into the shelter. Unlike the pristine and joyous looking photos on the website, in-person, the shelter was a bit overwhelming. Actually, a lot overwhelming. Photos were quiet and odorless. Life was loud. Louder than she'd expected, multiple dogs barked at her entry. The lobby stank of a combination of cleaning chemicals and the large quantity of animals all under one roof.

The shelter appeared to be smaller than it had in the photos, too. A couple rows of dogs on the left, cats on the right, all behind glass windows. A small reception and front desk area stood near the entrance. Three small, windowed rooms, each containing three blue plastic chairs, lined the wall behind it.

The inside was as empty of other people as the parking lot suggested. There were no employees bustling around, and no other potential adopters walked in after her. It was just her and a woman beaming from behind the front desk. The woman's dark brown eyes shone with excitement as Zuri approached. She looked close to Zuri's age, possibly younger. Long, straight black hair trailed loosely down her back. She wore jeans and a light blue T-shirt that read, TAILS ANIMAL SHELTER in bold black letters.

"Welcome to Tails Animal Shelter! My name's Julianna! Are you interested in a dog or a cat?" Julianna stood, and her shoulders barely cleared the desk's tall surface. Zuri wasn't that tall herself at five foot four, but this woman was barely over five feet.

"I'm here to see Max. He's a Husky I saw on your website." Zuri noticed the woman's eyes go from friendly to skeptical.

"Have you ever had a Husky before?" she questioned, raising an eyebrow.

"No, but I did some research online." Zuri tried to meet her gaze but ended up looking slightly past her.

"Huskies have a lot of energy. They're working dogs. Do you know anything about dog enrichment? Training? Do you run or do a lot of walking?" Julianna continued.

Enrichment? Zuri didn't even know what that meant. She also didn't run or even walk much these days. She sometimes worked out with online videos. Not recently, but sometimes. But plenty of non-active people had Huskies and other working dogs.

"I have a backyard," Zuri offered. Even to her own ears, it sounded flat and unimpressive.

"Yeah, a lot of people with backyards don't actually walk or do much with their dogs. Or at least that's what I've noticed, anyway. A backyard isn't enrichment or stimulation. It's just part of your house." She turned and motioned for Zuri to follow her into one of the windowed rooms past the desk.

Zuri felt her mouth go dry and a tightness in the pit of her stomach. She followed the unimpressed Julianna on autopilot, her brain too busy replaying what had gone wrong to notice her feet bringing her into one of the visiting rooms.

"So, if you won't let me adopt Max, what are we doing?" Zuri sat down in one of the blue plastic chairs.

"We'll find you someone." Julianna closed the door behind them.

"Don't I get to pick the dog I want?" Zuri's eyebrows knit together. Her fingernails scratched her thighs.

"Yeah, at a normal shelter, sure. But this is *Tails Animal Shelter*, where *we* choose the right furever friend for you," she said. "Our goal is to match the right pet to the right person to minimize the chance the animal will end up back in the shelter."

This was weird. It was a dog *Zuri*, not the shelter, was going to have to take care of and live with. Shouldn't she get to choose for herself? She wanted to get up and walk out, but as if guessing her thoughts, Julianna stayed plastered in front of the door, blocking her only exit.

"Name," Julianna demanded, grabbing a pen from beneath her clipboard's clip.

"Zuri Hansen," she answered reluctantly.

"Zuri. . ." The woman raised her clipboard and wrote her name down on the attached paper. "That's cute. And what do you do for a living, Zuri?" She stared down at her, pen in hand.

"I'm a website developer. I usually work from home." Zuri's hands fiddled with the rose quartz bead bracelet she wore around her wrist. She rubbed her fingers across the smooth beads and kept her gaze on the bridge of Julianna's nose. It was almost as if she were actually looking her in the eyes.

"Oh, that's great. Every animal we have here will love that. What are your hobbies?" Julianna asked brightly.

"I read a lot. And. . ." Zuri shrugged. "You know. Netflix."

"So, not active. Got it." Julianna wrote vigorously.

Harsh. So she wasn't an athlete, that didn't mean she was a complete couch potato. She had a standing desk and was thinking about getting one of those desk treadmills. Maybe.

"How do you feel about barking?"

"I don't like loud noises," Zuri confided. "But we've had a lot of break-ins in my neighborhood lately. I'd want the dog to let me know if someone was trying to get into my house. I'd prefer a big dog that might scare someone away."

Julianna tensed up again at Zuri's admission, and her eyes became cold.

"If you want a guard dog, that's something you're going to need to train a dog to do, no matter what dog you get. Some might just be better at it than others. Sometimes people come in looking for an aggressive dog to leave in their backyard, but we don't want our dogs living alone outside. They need love and attention."

"No, no," Zuri stammered. "I fully intend to have the dog live in my house with me. I already bought three dog beds. They're in my trunk if you want to see them."

She felt her face getting hot. This was not what she expected. None of the reviews she read online the night before mentioned being interrogated. Had Zuri known it was going to be like this, she would've chosen another shelter. This was what she got for making a life-changing decision in the middle of the night. She shouldn't have rushed. There were plenty of other places to adopt dogs, if she'd only done more research.

Julianna nodded, her face softening. She seemed to believe Zuri. That was something.

"Do you have people over at your house often? Does anyone else live in the home? Any other animals? Do you own or rent?" Julianna continued, rapid fire.

"Never. No, and no, it's just me. I own a condo," Zuri answered.

"Okay, sedentary, no social life." Julianna penned.

"Hey, I didn't say that." Zuri frowned, but Julianna ignored her.

Julianna's bluntness was beyond comprehension. Zuri didn't appreciate how she was characterizing her life. Other people might need more social outlets, but she enjoyed being alone. She was comfortable when she was alone. People drained her. This conversation alone would require hours of solitude before she could recover. Possibly days. Weeks even.

"Would you be willing to walk the dog at least three times a day? I know you have a backyard, but walking is good exercise and stimulation for the dog. And you. It would be good for you too."

"Absolutely," she replied, though she thought the last part was unnecessary. Walking more probably would be good for Zuri, but it wasn't any of Julianna's business.

"Okay." Julianna peered down at her clipboard. "Lonely, anxious, anti-social. Hmm."

"Hey, you can't—" she started, but Julianna cut her off.

"Oh! I know the perfect dog for you!" Julianna exclaimed. "Just promise to keep an open mind."

She didn't wait for Zuri to respond before leaving the small room.

How on earth was this woman still working here? Had no one complained about how rude she was?

Zuri thought about sneaking out while she had the chance, but her curiosity got the better of her. She wondered what kind of dog the rude woman could see her with. It was like a real-life version of a "What kind of dog are you?" quiz. She couldn't resist knowing the answer.

It didn't take long before Julianna was back with what she guessed was supposed to be the perfect dog for Zuri. She watched as the dog hurriedly walked in front of Julianna until she attempted to bring her into the small room. Then the dog panicked and tried to turn around. Julianna nearly had to drag it inside. Once the door was securely closed, she dropped the leash.

It wasn't Max.

This dog was black and large. Or it just looked large next to the petite shelter employee. It was fluffy, though a few bald patches revealed pink skin. Little pointy ears moved up in alarm as the dog's dark brown eyes searched for an alternate exit. A purple tongue hung from the dog's mouth as it panted. It didn't acknowledge Zuri at all.

"This is Gigi. She's a Chow Chow. Or at least mostly Chow. Probably. I think you two would be great together." Julianna grinned, clearly proud of herself.

"I don't remember seeing her on the website." She stared at Gigi, who gave up on an escape and went to the farthest corner of the room, away from both Julianna and Zuri, to lie down.

"She technically isn't up for adoption." Julianna's smile faltered for a second before she was beaming again. "I really think she can't miss out on the chance to go home with the right person, and I don't know if we'll find anyone else soon."

"What makes you think we'd be so great together? And aren't Chows supposed to be aggressive? Is she safe?" Zuri began fiddling with the beads on her bracelet again. It wasn't too late to go to a different shelter where she could pick out the dog herself, like she'd planned to.

"Does she look vicious to you?" Julianna impatiently waved a hand toward Gigi, who looked more scared and tired than anything else.

"Chows can be anti-social. They're like the introverts of the dog world. People just assume any dog that doesn't react like a Lab around people is aggressive." Julianna crossed her arms over her chest.

"People will think Gigi's mean and stay away, which is what you want, right? Wouldn't that alone make her a good fit since you're worried about someone breaking in?" Julianna continued.

"Well, yeah I guess, but—"

"Chows don't bark a lot. She's past the annoying adolescent phase. She's super chill. If you walk her a few times a day, she'll be good to hang with you while you read or whatever," Julianna cut her off again.

That sounded good. If she was honest with herself, she had been a little worried about how to keep a high energy dog entertained. Images of her couch in pieces flitted across her mind.

"What about those bald spots? Is she sick or something?" Zuri didn't want to take home a sick animal. While researching last night, she'd seen several posts on social media about expensive surprise vet bills for dogs recently taken home. She planned to get pet insurance to protect her savings, but no insurance company would cover a pre-existing condition.

"Our vet said she's healthy. They think it's just stress. You'll get a coupon for a free vet checkup when you take her too. She's already spayed, so you can take her home today."

"Can I think about it?" Zuri asked, not completely sold that this was the dog for her. Something about it didn't feel right.

"Look, if you don't take her today, like right now, they might euthanize her." Julianna's face fell.

"Euthanize her? Why?" Zuri's hands tightened into fists.

"She's a Chow. It's hard to adopt them out because of breed restrictions and, like I said, people *think* they're aggressive."

"But you have dozens of Pit Bulls," Zuri reasoned.

"Yeah, but they're super friendly and cuddly. How many people want to take home a dog who doesn't even approach them?" Julianna threw her hands toward Gigi again. The dog's eyes watched them nervously, but she didn't move.

"I don't know. . ." Zuri hesitated.

"She's perfect for you. You own your home so no breed restrictions to worry about. She looks intimidating, but I promise she isn't actually reactive to people or other dogs. I'm telling you, you will not find a more perfect dog for you. Trust me. I do this all day, every day. I can sense it!" Julianna exclaimed with conviction.

"If it doesn't work out, you can always bring her back. We would much rather people bring the dog back to us than dump it somewhere," Julianna quickly added.

Zuri took another glance over at Gigi, who didn't look particularly excited to be there. The thought of going to another shelter and having to prove she could take care of a dog again was unbearable. Although she hadn't considered adopting a Chow, if everything Julianna said was true, this might work. If it didn't, at least she could bring the dog back.

"Okay." She nodded.

Julianna literally jumped, raising her hands high above her head.

"You won't regret this, I promise!" she screamed, startling Gigi, who stood and backed up into the wall.

Julianna put a hand on the doorknob, causing Gigi to forget her fear and move toward the door. Julianna grabbed the leash.

"Pull up to the back and I'll bring her out to your car." Julianna opened the door.

"Don't I need to pay an adoption fee or sign something?" Zuri stood, but Julianna was already hurrying out the door.

"No, nope. Just get to the back ASAP." Julianna didn't wait before unlocking the hall door with her key card and urging Gigi through it.

Zuri did as instructed and pulled her car around to the rear of the building. Julianna didn't even wait for her to put it in park before opening the back door and urging Gigi to jump in. Once Julianna secured Gigi in the back seat, she slammed the door shut. She rolled down her window and Julianna thrusted a vet visit voucher and a packet of papers at her.

Literally at her. They almost collided with Zuri's face.

"You're good to go. Enjoy your new life as a dog mom." Julianna looked around before jogging back inside the building.

That was weird. Super weird. But what was Zuri going to do about it now? Gigi sat in the back seat, ready to go. She looked at Zuri expectantly as she panted. It almost looked like she was smiling, glad to be free from dog jail.

"Okay, I guess we're doing this," Zuri mumbled, mostly to herself.

Chapter 3

Zuri wasn't sure if she had adopted a dog or a very realistic looking stuffed one.

After taking Gigi inside and letting her explore her new home, Zuri went back to the car and brought in all the dog supplies she purchased. It took three trips. She placed a dog bed in her office, at the foot of her bed, and in a corner in the living room near the couch. Heaving the giant bag of dog food through the living room, she dropped it on the kitchen floor with an enormous thump that caused Gigi to shuffle in the opposite direction.

Sighing to herself, she admitted the rude shelter employee, Julianna, was right. She needed to workout. Once upon a time, she had been fairly active. In high school and college, her primary means of transportation were her roller skates since she wasn't patient enough to wait for the bus and skates took up less room and were easier to move than a bike. She took them everywhere. Even her first job in high school was as a carhop at a Sonic.

It had been a long time since she'd worn them, but they were probably around somewhere. Maybe she should skate over to a gym.

Zuri washed the food and water bowls and put them on the floor next to the kitchen island. She filled the water bowl with filtered water from her pitcher. It was a little extra, but unfiltered Arizona water, at least where she lived, tasted like dirt. Gigi didn't deserve to drink dirt water, even if she didn't notice the taste.

Looking over at the large fluffy black dog laying in the living room, she realized she had forgotten something important.

"Sorry Gigi, I should introduce myself. I'm Zuri. Zuri Hansen," Zuri said from a few feet away.

Gigi responded with a blank, almost bored looking stare.

"So do you want to stay a Gigi, or would you like a new name to go with your new home?"

Blank stare.

"How about. . ." Zuri paused, trying to think of a name befitting her new furry housemate. The shape of the dog's head and her black fur kind of reminded her of King, a character from an animated show she adored.

"How about King?" Zuri asked. The dog heaved a snort-like sigh. "Queen? Since you're a girl?"

This time, the dog closed her eyes.

"Okay, so you like Gigi?" Zuri asked, and when the dog opened her eyes, Zuri felt like it was decided. "Gigi it is."

Zuri added some dry food to the new food bowl, but Gigi never got up to eat. During the three hours since they arrived home, Gigi mostly stayed in the living room, in her dog bed, immobile. She watched the door and kept an eye on Zuri but otherwise didn't move. The dog remained so still that if she didn't know better, she might have thought Gigi was a decoration.

Google suggested she give Gigi some time to get comfortable in the new space. To use food to get Gigi to associate her as a friend, not a foe. Zuri brought some wet food over and tried spooning it near Gigi's mouth, but she moved her nose and face away from the spoon. She tried the dog treats and dry food, but nothing interested the stoic dog. She even grabbed some peanut butter from the fridge, and after making sure it was just peanuts, tried that too, but Gigi shunned both her and the peanut butter.

She tried petting Gigi on the head gently. When she didn't growl or move away, she carefully pet her a few more times. Gigi was soft, her thick black hair smooth under Zuri's hand. She needed a bath and a good brushing, but now that Zuri was over her initial shock of leaving the shelter with a Chow and not a

Husky, her initial anxiety was waning. The dog just needed some TLC.

Moving to the couch, Zuri gave Gigi some space. She wasted hours the night before researching Huskies. Now she needed to learn everything she could about Chows.

Julianna warned her that Chows were introverts. Not exactly the friendly and attention seeking type of dog Zuri was familiar with. While she waited for Gigi to warm up to her, she watched videos of other Chows on social media. With their owners, they strutted about, tails wagging and joy in their eyes, a stark contrast to Gigi's thus far Eeyore-like personality.

Julianna had said that if it didn't work out, Zuri could bring Gigi back. Nonetheless, the thought of taking Gigi back to the shelter made her slightly nauseous. This dog had clearly been through something. Gigi's last owner might have been abusive and that could have been why she was so tightly wound. Or maybe they had just fallen on hard times and Gigi felt depressed at being separated from the only family she had ever known. Zuri could come up with a thousand scenarios to explain Gigi's demeanor, but she was responsible for Gigi now. She was determined to do her best. She wouldn't throw her away.

Looking again at Gigi's mussy black fur sticking out in a few places, she researched dog grooming. It surprised Zuri that the shelter hadn't done more to clean her up. The dogs online all looked like they were in excellent condition. The whole situation at the shelter was unusual. Her stomach still twisted in knots at the memory of Julianna rushing her out without even getting any of her information. Definitely not normal.

Zuri eventually stopped worrying and researching to leaf through the papers Julianna had left with her. She went online and scheduled a vet appointment at Paws and Claws. Luckily, they had an opening for that Friday. They were offering a free checkup with the voucher. Like the shelter, it was nearby. The reviews were positive. Mostly. A few complaints about overcharging here and there. One reviewer accused the clinic of killing their iguana. . .

A soft rumbling noise made Zuri almost leap off the couch. She looked toward Gigi's bed. Unable to stay alert any longer, the dog had fallen asleep. Her snores continued to rumble through the living room. That would certainly take some getting used to. Especially if Gigi decided to sleep in Zuri's room at night. Julianna should have given her some earplugs.

Unfortunately, the loud blaring ring of Zuri's phone cut the nap short.

The name Mom flashed on Zuri's phone screen. She blamed Donna for asking about her family the day before and reminding the universe that it had been far too long since her peace was shattered.

"Hello?" Zuri answered.

She felt her shoulders inching toward her ears as every muscle in her body tensed.

"Hi honey, it's been a while, so I thought I'd call." Noise in the background muffled her mother's voice. The mingled voices of a crowd paired with the faint melody of a song she vaguely remembered hearing on the radio.

Honey. Now that she knew what kind of call it was going to be, she tried to relax a little.

"Where are you?" Zuri wasn't really interested in the answer, but she knew, even if she didn't ask, her mother would tell her. Their conversations were usually one-sided.

"At the airport. I'm heading to see your grandparents, but don't tell them. It's a surprise."

Translation: her mother had broken up with her latest boyfriend, whom she had been living with, and was going to stay at her grandparents' house until she found somewhere else to go.

"I haven't talked to them in years," Zuri reminded her.

Her mother's parents had never liked Zuri's father. She was also pretty sure her mother was their least favorite child. While her mother was what they referred to as "a mess," their favorite child, her Uncle Nick, was an even bigger mess, at least in her opinion. Needless to say, no one cared about her opinion.

It had been obvious to her growing up that they favored their other grandchildren over her. Sure, she got birthday cards, but they never came to visit her or called like they did her cousins. Even during the brief periods of time she'd lived with them over school breaks or summers so her mother could gallivant into a new relationship child free, there was always an invisible wall between her and her grandparents. A line drawn in the sand. She wasn't sure if it was her they didn't like, her parents, or a combination of the two.

"You should call them," her mother chided.

"Did you need something? When does your flight board?" Zuri deflected. They weren't having this argument again. If her grandparents wanted to talk to her, they had her number.

"Right." Her mother took a breath. Here it was. "I was hoping you could lend me some money. Just this once. I promise I'll pay you back."

"How much do you need?" Zuri bit her cheeks to keep from sighing. It had only been six months since the last time her mother had "borrowed" money.

Her mother remained quiet on the other end, the noise from the busy airport in the background filling the silence.

"How much?" Zuri repeated, trying to keep her voice as neutral and judgment free as possible. She probably wasn't doing a good job.

"Three thousand," her mother admitted.

"What?" Zuri gaped. "Mom, I can't afford to give you that kind of money!"

"You have at least five times that in the bank. I know you do," her mom said accusingly. A flip had been switched.

"Yeah, and I have plans for that money." Zuri felt her tongue scrape her canines as she tried to keep herself calm, to keep her voice level and emotionless.

"I always pay you back. Just let me borrow it," her mom asked again.

"What do you even need three thousand dollars for?" Zuri knew she would not get the full answer, but she figured some was better than none.

"I just got behind on a few bills. That's all." Zuri could hear her mother's tight-lipped line of a smile through the phone.

"I can send you a few hundred that you don't have to pay back, but I can't give you that much money, Mom. Not right now. Plus, I just got a dog and already spent way more on her than I was planning." Zuri sighed.

"Why did you get a dog? You're not even a dog person. You never liked any of the dogs we had when you were growing up," her mother snarled.

That was true. But they had all been little yappy dogs who peed all over the apartments and followed her mother from room to room. None of them had lasted a year before they were given away or the door was *accidentally* left open and they ran off, never to be found again.

"Just because I didn't like the dogs you picked out doesn't mean I don't like dogs." Zuri closed her eyes. She didn't have the energy to argue. Not after the sleepless night or strange shelter visit.

"Send me a picture," her mother demanded. Zuri actually hadn't taken any pictures of Gigi yet. Rather than argue, now seemed as good of a time as any. She pulled herself off the couch and crouched in front of Gigi, who eyed her phone camera wearily. She quickly snapped a picture and sent it to her mother before retreating to the couch.

"Isn't that a Chow?" her mother stated more than asked. "Those dogs can kill you. You should return it."

Zuri rolled her eyes.

"Even if I did, I still wouldn't have three thousand dollars to send you, Mom," Zuri stated, moving the conversation back to the real reason for her mother's call.

"Don't bother sending anything, then." Her mother sniffed. "You've always been so selfish. Don't call me crying when that dog bites you, either."

Her mother hung up.

Sinking back against the couch cushions, Zuri pulled up her banking app and sent her mother three hundred, not three thousand dollars. A tenth of what she'd asked for. Her old therapist would give her a disapproving look, but Zuri couldn't help it. If her mother was desperate enough to ask, she couldn't help but give. It was toxic, and she knew it. Her mother would be fine whether she sent her money or not. She was always fine. The real reason Zuri sent the money was because if she didn't send something, she would feel guilty. If she sent the money, she still felt like crap, but less guilty. A lose-lose situation.

Zuri looked over at Gigi, still snug in her luxury dog bed. Gigi looked back.

"I know dogs have excellent hearing, so assuming you heard any of that, just ignore her. I'm not returning you. You're stuck with me."

Chapter 4

Friday

Zuri sat upright, her thumb absently rubbing the leash in her hands. Gigi looked up at her nervously, her head and front paws peeking out from underneath the plastic chair where she hid. Clean, her coat shiny and brushed, she looked like a new dog.

Nervous that the vet and staff would think she was a bad dog mom, she took Gigi to the groomers that morning before her checkup. At first Gigi wouldn't walk behind the counter with the groomer, so Zuri had pretended to walk with her for a few steps. When Gigi noticed Zuri hadn't gone through the door to the back with her, she'd given her the most pointed and accusing glare Zuri had ever seen in a dog's eyes. If looks could kill. . .

The groomer had a window where pet parents could watch, but seeing Gigi's little legs quake in fear was too stressful for Zuri. She'd walked around the adjoined pet shop instead, looking for a reward for Gigi's good behavior. Since food didn't seem to interest Gigi, she grabbed a stuffed toy shaped like a duck and another shaped like a coffee cup, hoping the dog would like at least one of them.

A pink collar with darker pink flowers caught her eye. She added it to the cart without a second thought. Under it on the shelf was a matching harness. She grabbed an extra-large, hoping it would fit. The shelter had given Gigi a flimsy collar, but it was frayed and dirty. There was no telling how much longer it would last.

Only when she'd gotten to the register did she realize she should have paid more attention. While the harness was just a harness, the collar wasn't a regular collar. A small, dime-sized GPS chip came embedded near the clasp. It cost three times more than what Zuri had expected. Gigi didn't really need a GPS collar, but she was too embarrassed to ask the cashier to void the purchase. It didn't help that she got the text from the groomer that Gigi was ready to be picked up right as she was checking out either. At least it was pretty.

"Gigi?" called a vet tech from the back door.

"We're here." Zuri stood and Gigi followed suit. This time Gigi walked behind Zuri though, instead of in front of her. Smarty-pants.

"Aw, she looks like a little bear," the vet tech cooed before leading them to a small room.

"The doctor will be in soon. Let's get her weight." She pointed to a large floor scale.

Zuri coaxed Gigi to get on the scale. Gigi surprisingly obliged, but she kept her eyes trained on the vet tech. Anytime the woman took a step in Gigi's direction, she backed up.

"Fifty-four pounds," the tech wrote down Gigi's weight. "I'm going to get her temperature. Can you hold her?"

"Sure," Zuri replied on autopilot, a little off guard. While Gigi didn't seem to mind her putting on her leash or petting her, Zuri had mostly tried to give the dog her space. She gently took a light hold of Gigi's neck. When the dog squirmed at the vet tech's touch, she tightened her grip.

The vet tech successfully got Gigi's temperature and left the room to inform the doctor that they were ready.

Zuri moved to sit in one of the chairs, and Gigi followed, diving beneath her once more. She leaned over and ran her hand between Gigi's ears. First the groomer and then the vet, two places no dog ever wanted to go. Hopefully, Gigi wouldn't hate her after today. It would suck if her own dog didn't like her. Not that she was sure Gigi liked her much to begin with.

It didn't take long for the door to open again. A thin woman, a couple inches taller than Zuri, walked in. She had short dark brown hair, pulled back in a low hanging ponytail. A few strands framed her face, hanging just below her jaw. Her matching dark brown eyes looked curiously from Zuri to Gigi beneath her bangs.

"You're right, she looks just like a bear," the woman turned to say to the vet tech, who rejoined the room and closed the door again.

"I'm Dr. Rodriguez," the woman said to Zuri, holding her hand out for a handshake.

Zuri took her hand and shook it awkwardly. Handshakes were not her favorite thing. She always worried her hands were sweaty, or clammy, or both.

"This is Gigi and her new mom, Zuri," the vet tech introduced them.

"Oh, I'm not her mom. Her caretaker I guess," Zuri replied.

"Caretaker?" Dr. Rodriguez raised an eyebrow. "So, she's not your dog?"

"No, she's mine." Zuri was confused.

"Then you're her mom." Dr. Rodriguez got down on the floor in front of Gigi, pulling some treats out of her pocket.

"Oh," she exclaimed, finally understanding what the doctor was getting at. "I just don't like calling myself her mom. Because you know, I'm not actually her mom. I like to think of us more like friends or roommates."

Dr. Rodriguez snorted a little before she smiled at Gigi, offering her a treat.

"I love her collar and the matching harness. It's cute," Dr. Rodriguez stated. "I see you're here for a check-up. Is there anything you're concerned about?"

"I haven't been able to get her to eat anything. I adopted her a few days ago and all she'll have is water."

The doctor's smile turned into a straight line.

"Has she had any bowel movements?"

"She's peed, but hasn't gone number two," Zuri answered.

"Any vomiting, trying to vomit, or has she been licking the roof of her mouth a lot?"

Zuri shook her head.

"Can you try walking over here? I'd like to examine her abdomen. I need her to stand up." Dr. Rodriguez stood and stepped a few feet back, giving Gigi some space. The vet tech did the same.

Zuri stood and walked in front of the door the vet tech had come through from the back of the office. Gigi looked at her in panic and scrambled out from under the chair to follow. When she reached her, Zuri knelt down and pet Gigi on the head.

"It's okay Gigi, the doctor's just going to check you out."

Dr. Rodriguez knelt down next to Gigi again, placing her hand out for the dog to sniff. Gigi stared at it and then turned to look at Zuri as if to say, *is she for real?*

The doctor slowly pet Gigi on the head and scratched behind her ears. When Gigi didn't snap at her or growl, she moved her hands down her body and felt around her stomach and abdomen. Zuri kept her hands around Gigi's neck just in case.

"Everything feels normal." She paused, looking at the bald spots in Gigi's fur. "Did she have these when you got her?"

"Yes."

"Can you try opening her mouth? I just want to look at her gums."

"You want me to do it?" Zuri questioned.

"Chows are usually better handled by their owners. While she's been good so far, I don't want to put her at risk of getting an unnecessary bite on her record. She seems to trust you, and I just need a quick peek."

Zuri was not as confident as the doctor that Gigi trusted her, though she didn't think Gigi would bite her. So far, during their time together, she hadn't done anything that could remotely be considered aggressive. Nervously, she complied with the request and gently opened Gigi's mouth. Gigi wasn't happy about it and tried to shake Zuri's hands off her face, but she eventually caved and stayed still.

"I don't see any broken teeth and her gums look good. How old is she?" Dr. Rodriguez asked.

"I don't know. They didn't give me a lot of information at the shelter." Zuri shrugged.

"Which shelter?"

"Tails."

"They usually try to get a lot of information out of previous owners." Dr. Rodriguez looked puzzled.

"To be honest, it was really weird. She didn't even take any of my information before putting Gigi in the back of my car. At least, nothing that's usually important." Zuri frowned.

"Julianna?" A light of recognition went off in Dr. Rodriguez's eyes.

"Yeah. I think that was her name," Zuri mumbled.

"I've known her for a while. She does this sometimes. If they're full and going to transfer a dog into a bigger shelter or consider euthanasia, she sometimes just gives animals away." The doctor stood and went to the computer on the wall next to the exam table. She began typing her findings into Gigi's chart.

"And they haven't fired her?"

"She's a volunteer." Dr. Rodriguez shrugged, continuing to type.

Zuri didn't know what to say. It was still weird that the shelter hadn't banned her or something. Didn't they need the adoption fees? Wasn't this a liability issue?

"I'd guess Gigi's about five or six years old, but you can buy a DNA test kit that will give you some more information."

"Why won't she eat?"

"We can do an X-ray to check for a blockage and maybe run some blood work, but it could just be that she's still getting used to her new home. Have you tried chicken or something high value?"

"Just wet food, dry food, peanut butter, and some pizza crust last night, but she turned up her nose to everything."

"We'll get you an estimate for the X-ray and you can decide what you want to do."

"What do you recommend?" Zuri said, not worried about the cost. Gigi's insurance wouldn't kick in yet, but Zuri's tech job provided her with a cushion for emergencies.

"I think you should take her home and try some higher value foods first. She doesn't seem to be in pain and otherwise looks pretty healthy. You've only had her a few days, and we don't know what kind of situation she came from. It can take dogs a while to adjust."

"What about the bald spots?" That wasn't normal, in Zuri's unprofessional opinion.

"It's not uncommon for dogs to develop bald spots when they're in a stressful environment for long periods of time. Did Julianna say how long she'd been at the shelter?"

"No, she didn't really tell me much at all. This dog definitely wasn't on their website, though. Julianna had to go to the back of the shelter to get her."

Dr. Rodriguez pursed her lips and scowled. She sighed before turning to her computer and typing in a few more notes.

"I don't think it's anything serious. She hasn't been scratching at the spots, has she?"

"No." She hadn't, Zuri realized.

Dr. Rodriguez locked the computer and turned to Zuri. "For today, I just recommend giving her some basic vaccines. We can and should also do a heartworm test. We'll call you, and if she's negative, you can get her on a heartworm prevention. Because of the hair loss and lack of appetite, we can do some blood work if you want. If she still hasn't eaten in a couple days after you try something higher value or her mood seems to decline, bring her back and we'll do an X-ray."

All of that seemed to make sense. Zuri appreciated that they weren't pushing the most expensive tests or trying to sell her stuff she didn't need.

"Okay. Let's do that." Zuri nodded, still feeling a little nervous.

She was responsible for Gigi and wanted to make sure she was okay. If Gigi didn't eat soon and she later found out she was sick or in pain, Zuri was going to feel extremely guilty.

"Great. Michelle will bring you an estimate for the work we'll do today and another for the potential X-ray, and once you sign off, we'll take Gigi to the back to draw some blood. We can give her the vaccines while she's back there. Just rabies, Bordetella, Lepto, and Distemper."

"Distemper?" Zuri had to have misheard her. There was a vaccine against the dog having a bad temper?

"It's a highly contagious disease that attacks the dog's nervous system. Is this your first dog?" Dr. Rodriguez questioned, looking mildly concerned now.

"Yes. My first as an adult on my own, anyway."

"And you picked a Chow?" Dr. Rodriguez said in disbelief.

"I didn't pick her. Julianna insisted I take her. She took the 'We choose the right furever friend for you' thing very seriously," Zuri said.

It was what it was. In hindsight, maybe she should have just left and gone to another shelter to pick her own dog. On the other hand, Gigi not eating aside, they had been getting along pretty well.

So far, she was low maintenance and independent. She didn't bother Zuri while she was working, loved lounging in the backyard during the cooler parts of the day and didn't yank Zuri's arm unless she saw a lizard or rabbit, so their walks were leisurely and enjoyable. Zuri had to give Julianna some credit for the choice. She certainly hadn't been too far off the mark. It also didn't hurt that Gigi was adorable, especially after a bath and a little brushing, despite the bald spots.

Now that she was out and about more, she had also seen a few Huskies in the wild. The energy. The friendliness. It would have been too much for her.

"I'm gonna kill her." She heard Dr. Rodriguez mumble under her breath before she turned back to her computer.

Heat rushed to her neck and shoulders, and the weight of a rock suddenly hit her stomach. Her breath quickened to keep up with her beating heart as a wave of thoughts fought for space in her mind.

Zuri didn't like the idea of anyone, but especially a veterinarian, thinking she was a bad dog owner. She followed all the rules. She kept Gigi on a leash at all times and would pick up after her if she ever decided to go number two. Like Julianna insisted, they went on regular walks throughout the day, and she even washed her ceramic water bowl in the dishwasher nightly. The groomer had recommended a few different brushes and grooming supplies that Zuri had purchased immediately, not even waiting to see if she could find them cheaper online. Did she miss something?

"Am I not a good enough dog owner?" Zuri asked, a little afraid of hearing the answer.

"No, no!" Dr. Rodriguez immediately recounted. "It's just that Chows can be stubborn and independent, so they're not known to be a great choice for a first-time dog owner."

"She is a little stubborn," Zuri admitted. "But we're also both a little introverted, so maybe that's why we seem to get along. At least so far."

"That's great." Dr. Rodriguez didn't meet her eyes. She combed through her bangs before walking to the door. "Michelle will be in shortly with the estimate."

Zuri looked down at Gigi as the door closed behind Dr. Rodriguez.

"We're doing just fine. Aren't we?"

Gigi went back to her hiding spot underneath the chair and sighed at Zuri, dropping her head down onto the floor. It wasn't a resounding yes, but it wasn't a no. She sat back down, hoping they could get out of there soon. In the meantime, she registered Gigi's expensive new collar. It was something to do, which would help keep her spiraling thoughts in check, and she also might as well get her money's worth.

Chapter 5

Saturday

Chicken. Ground turkey. Ground beef. Pizza. Chinese food. The dog wouldn't eat anything. Zuri tilted her head back and groaned while she waited for Gigi to finish sniffing a bush. At her wit's end, she didn't know what to try next.

The day before, while waiting for Gigi to get her blood work and vaccines done, Zuri ordered some groceries to be delivered that night. She cooked the chicken by boiling it in plain water, but Gigi wasn't even remotely tempted.

She thought it was possible Gigi just needed time to decompress from the vet. She tried again later, but Gigi merely rolled her eyes. Most dogs didn't roll their eyes, but Gigi did, Zuri was sure of it.

That morning she tried again with ground beef and turkey, but no luck. At lunch they took a car ride and drove through McDonald's, but Gigi was not impressed with her happy meal. At least Zuri got to eat the fries.

Gigi yanked on the leash, pulling Zuri out of her thoughts. Cars took up all the extra space along the street in front of the house on the corner. The smell of grilled beef filled the air.

Gigi tried to pull Zuri up to her neighbor's back gate, but Zuri pulled back on the leash. She didn't know this neighbor, and as a black person in a mostly white neighborhood, she needed to be careful.

"Gigi, let's go," she called, but the Chow sat in front of the gate and stared longingly, whining; a sound she had yet to hear her dog ever make.

Suddenly, the gate opened. Before Zuri could pull Gigi away, a tall gray-haired man walked out, pushing a large black trash can. He stopped in his tracks, eyes taking them in.

"Well, hello there. And who's this?" He pushed the trash can to the side and stepped closer to Gigi. She didn't shy away like she did with most people. Instead she stared at the man, cocking her head attentively to the side.

"Sorry, I think my dog smelled your BBQ. She's refused to eat anything, so maybe I need to get some of whatever you have on your grill." She gently tugged on the leash again, attempting to get Gigi to stand.

"I have a few steaks on there right now. Let me go get a piece for her." The man turned around, gate slamming behind him before Zuri could stop him. He was back in less than a minute with a few pieces of cut up steak on a plastic plate.

With no hesitation, Gigi devoured every piece and licked the plate clean of all its juices. Zuri's eyes widened in both relief and horror. Would Gigi really only eat steak? That couldn't be healthy, not in the long run. For now, at least she would eat something.

"Wow, I haven't been able to get her to eat anything all week. Thanks!" Zuri paused. "Sorry, I don't think we've met. I'm Zuri. I live on the other side over there. Next to Donna, if you know her." She pointed.

"Who doesn't know Donna!" He smiled. "I'm Paul. We used to have a black Chow just like this years ago."

Paul grinned at Gigi before picking up the plate. Gigi backed up and politely sat in front of Zuri. She seemed relaxed, but her eyes danced between Paul and the empty plate.

"Oh, really? This is my first one. I got her from Tails." Zuri rocked back on her heels. Small talk was her enemy, but the man had just fed her dog steak, so she had to try.

"Tails. I know that place. We got our last dog from there. Strange how they insist on picking out the dog for you, but she was one of the best dogs we've ever had."

"Yeah, it was weird at first for me too, but it looks like it worked out."

Gigi, apparently giving up on getting seconds, got up and started pulling Zuri away.

"I guess we're going now. Thanks for the steak. Apparently, that's what she's been holding out for." Zuri smiled.

"Anytime. Congratulations on the new dog." He smiled and waved before going back into his own yard.

She had lived in this neighborhood for a couple of years, and except for Donna, never really talked to any of her neighbors. Everything she knew mostly came second hand from the nosy woman. A week with Gigi, and she was having an actual conversation with one. She still didn't enjoy talking to nosy Donna, but Paul wasn't bad. Maybe he could give her some advice if Gigi kept being stubborn about eating.

She remembered playing with the neighborhood kids when she was in elementary school. No matter where they'd moved, there were always other kids, and they were as eager for someone to play with as she had been. The older she got though, the less she talked to her neighbors. It was a truth universally acknowledged that middle school girls were mean. High school girls weren't much nicer. That was when she'd started keeping to herself.

When they got home, Zuri ordered steak from her grocery delivery app, along with a few indulgences for herself. She deserved a reward for talking to her neighbor, after all.

Chapter 6

Sunday

Zuri walked Gigi down their usual route. She eventually wanted to take her to the park, but not until she was eating properly. There was definitely a little more pep in Gigi's step after eating a small amount of steak for dinner and breakfast that morning.

This was their third stroll for the day and Zuri intended to keep it short as the afternoon heat baked the city. She made a habit of checking the sidewalk before they went out, and although it was only warm and not hot, she tried to encourage Gigi to walk in the grass when it was available. Gigi, of course, had her own ideas about this and preferred to stay on the sidewalk. If Zuri tried to shorten the leash to keep Gigi in the grass, Gigi would tug on the leash, yanking Zuri forward until they were on the sidewalk again. She was stubborn and wanted to live on her own terms.

When Gigi sniffed a spot she often peed on, Zuri thought little of it, until Gigi squatted. It differed from how she squatted when she was going to pee. Her back was round, and she took little steps, hobbling around in circles.

Finally, she was going to poop!

She pulled a plastic bag from her still-very-brand-new-looking dog poop bag holder.

Gigi whimpered, and a few drops of blood splashed onto the ground beneath her. Finally, she seemed to empty her bowels, but it wasn't doo-doo. Where she had squatted were four rather large gold coins, all covered in drops of bright red blood.

"What the. . ." She stared at the coins and then looked at Gigi who had laid herself down in the nearby grass. Blood rushed into Zuri's ears and she had to remind herself to breathe. There was no need to panic. She would not panic. Gigi was going to be fine. It was just a little blood. Tiny. Miniscule. Nothing to worry about. They could go to the vet and get this sorted out.

She picked up the coins with the plastic bag and tied it off with a knot, then grabbed another bag and double bagged the coins before sliding them into the back pocket of her shorts. It wasn't poop, but it had still come out of Gigi's butt. Gold or not, until the coins were swashed and maybe even after, they were gross.

Gigi was reluctant to get up so she pet her and let her rest for a few more minutes before insisting they walk back home. She didn't want Gigi to get overheated in addition to whatever this was.

The first thing Zuri did when they got back inside was call the vet. It was getting close to their closing time, so they might not see Gigi, but it was worth calling before she went to an emergency vet. She wasn't worried about the care costing more, but the emergency vet was farther, and Gigi was uncomfortable, Zuri could tell. Instead of laying down in her own bed next to the couch or on the floor nearby like she usually did, Gigi got up on the couch and laid next to Zuri. Right next to Zuri. Not even the other side of the couch. Not normal at all.

"Claws and Paws Veterinary Clinic. How can I help you?" the receptionist answered, her fake pleasant customer service voice grating against Zuri's ear.

"Hi, I was there with my dog, Gigi, the day before yesterday for our first checkup, but she just pooped these weird gold coins and some blood. Is there any way you could see her before you close today?"

"I'm not sure we'll be able to fit you in but let me go check with the vet. Who did your dog see when you were here before?"

"Dr. Rodriguez, I think. Dark hair in a ponytail. A little tall. Pretty." Zuri hadn't meant to add the last part. Was it weird to think your dog's vet was pretty? It was just an objective observation. Hopefully, the receptionist wouldn't think to mention it to Dr.

Rodriguez. At least she hadn't accidentally said *a little mean.*

"Yeah, that's Dr. Rodriguez." Zuri could almost hear the receptionist nodding. "She's here today. Hold on and I'll see if I can pencil you in."

Seconds that felt like hours ticked by.

"Are you still there?" The receptionist rejoined the call.

"Yes!" Zuri answered, a little too loud.

"Dr. Rodriguez said she would see you after her last patient if you can get here in the next thirty minutes."

"Yes! We're only a couple of minutes away. We'll be right there. Thank you so much."

"No problem. We'll see you soon," the receptionist chimed before hanging up.

"Come on Gigi, we're going to the vet." Zuri stood. Gigi looked at her but made no move to get up. She went to the door and got her leash and harness. Still as a statue, Gigi didn't even blink.

"Gigi, let's go," she squealed in a high-pitched voice that dogs were supposed to like but made her feel ridiculous. Gigi closed her eyes, unamused and unimpressed.

Surprising both of them, Zuri went to the couch and wrapped her arms around Gigi, scooping her up. It wasn't her best idea. She wobbled a little before placing the dog on the floor, panting. Gigi still refused to stand, knowing full well just how heavy she was.

Zuri opened the front door, walked to her car, and opened the door to the back seat. She went back to the living room and once again, heaved the hefty Gigi up and carried her to the car. Barely. Gigi didn't help her one bit, but at least she didn't wiggle in her arms either.

After frantically grabbing her wallet, phone, and keys and locking up the house, they were on their way.

Chapter 7

Zuri sat in a plastic chair, tapping her right foot anxiously. Any minute now, Dr. Rodriguez would bring Gigi back from her X-ray. Although they hadn't made time to call Zuri yet, when she arrived, they let her know Gigi's blood work from the other day came back normal.

At first, Dr. Rodriguez had assumed the coins were Zuri's, and told her, "You have to watch dogs carefully. Sometimes they eat things they shouldn't."

"I'm not a coin collector," Zuri had stated, trying not to sound defensive. "The coins aren't mine. She must've eaten them before I picked her up from the shelter."

Dr. Rodriguez didn't exactly apologize for her assumption, but her face went a little red. She had carried on as if she hadn't accused Zuri of being an irresponsible pet owner. It was nice of the doctor to see Gigi on such short notice and to stay late, but if she kept assuming things about them, Zuri was going to have to find a different vet.

"Here's your mom," Michelle, the same vet tech who had helped them the last time, chimed as she led Gigi back into their exam room. Gigi hurriedly shuffled right up to Zuri as her tail swung back and forth behind her.

"We didn't have to sedate her. She stayed perfectly still." Michelle smiled.

"Thank you." Zuri took the leash from Michelle.

"It's going to be a few minutes, and then Dr. Rodriguez will be in."

Zuri nodded in response, and Michelle left the room again.

Gigi laid down at Zuri's feet, heaving an enormous sigh. Zuri reached down and ran her fingers through her dog's thick fur. A wave of guilt swept over her like a much too heavy weighted blanket. She didn't like to see Gigi so distressed.

The door swung open and a blonde woman dressed in a white coat over purple scrubs walked in. A glimmer from a large gold ring with a red ruby gemstone on her right index finger caught Zuri's attention. It seemed odd for someone who put on and took off gloves all day to bother with a ring, especially one that looked so expensive.

She recognized the woman as another vet from the clinic's website, though she couldn't remember her name. The woman's coffee-colored eyes flicked from Gigi to Zuri and her red lips shifted from a sharp line to a serene smile. A shiver ran down Zuri's spine. Something about this woman gave her the creeps. She instinctively sat up and shortened the leash, not enough to pull on Gigi's harness, but enough that if Gigi got up, she wouldn't be able to go far.

"Hello there. What an adorable matching harness and collar. I don't think I've seen this one before." The veterinarian stooped down in front of Gigi. The dog sat up slowly and she heard a low growl as Gigi flashed her teeth in warning.

"Um, we're already being helped by Dr. Rodriguez." Zuri grabbed the handle on Gigi's harness, just in case. She felt her shoulders inching toward her ears. There was just something about this woman that made her want to put some distance between them, but there was nowhere to go. Maybe it was her perfume. It was something flowery and sickeningly sweet. It didn't smell bad, but it was overpowering in the small room and something about it gave Zuri the urge to plug her nose.

"I was told these were yours?" The woman reached into her pocket and pulled out the four gold coins that Gigi had passed. They were clean now, no longer dripping with blood. It got stranger the more Zuri thought about it. There had been nothing but gold and blood when the techs unwrapped the coins to see what Gigi had passed. She didn't remember seeing any actual poop on the grass either. *Only blood and gold.*

When she was a kid, one of her mother's little dogs ate some of a doll's plastic clothing and eventually it came out with the dog's poop. The same thing had happened with crayons and other small miscellaneous items. If only the coins had come out, was it possible they had damaged Gigi's organs? Or did the steak help move things along, but it hadn't been digested yet? She really hoped Dr. Rodriguez came back soon with some answers.

"Yes." Zuri held her hand out to take the coins, and the woman's smile turned into a frown.

After waiting for what felt like a beat too long, she finally deposited them into Zuri's hand.

"The tech said your dog. . ." She paused, clearly looking for a more elegant choice of words.

"She pooped them," Zuri filled in.

"Right." The woman nodded. "How long have you had this dog, and where did you get her?"

Before Zuri could answer, Dr. Rodriguez knocked and opened the door without waiting for an answer. Her expression went from neutral to troubled as soon as she laid eyes on the newcomer.

"Dr. Smith, what are you doing here?" she questioned, clearly confused. "I thought you would've gone home by now."

"I was curious about where the coins came from, Claudia." Dr. Smith stood and smiled with all her teeth, which looked very sharp and almost shark-like. The smile didn't reach her eyes.

Claudia. Dr. Rodriguez's first name didn't escape Zuri's notice. She looked like a Claudia, especially when her dark hair was down like it was now. It framed her face before curling in just above her shoulders. She pulled it behind her ear as she signed into the computer, revealing small gold hoop earrings.

"I didn't know you were interested in coins." Dr. Rodriguez raised an eyebrow.

"Yes. I am a collector actually, so I wanted to see where they came from." Dr. Smith leaned against the exam table, looking anything but relaxed. Her smile turned into a line and her eyes flicked between Gigi, Zuri, and Dr. Rodriguez.

"I would like to discuss the results of the X-ray with my patient, Gigi, and her. . ." Dr. Rodrigues paused. "Her caretaker, Zuri, if you don't mind."

Dr. Rodriguez turned away from her computer and looked at Dr. Smith pointedly.

"I don't mind," Dr. Smith said, but she made no move to walk to the door.

"I meant you should go home, Dr. Smith," Dr. Rodriguez stated, point blank.

"Right." Dr. Smith straightened. "Well, it was nice to meet you Zuri, and Gigi." She tried to reach down to pet Gigi, but Gigi barked and snapped at her hand, just missing it by a quarter inch.

Grabbing the harness a little tighter, she looked up at Dr. Smith, expecting her to be startled or scared. She certainly was. Not of Gigi, but of the just barely missed consequences of her dog biting someone.

Instead, the woman looked down at the dog with more scorn and disdain than Zuri thought possible. Normally, Gigi was adorable, especially now that she was cleaned up, in her matching pink floral collar and harness. How could anyone look at her with such pure hatred? Especially a veterinarian. To do this job day in and day out, you would have to love animals a lot, and at least be able to tolerate people. Didn't this kind of thing occasionally happen to them? It shouldn't have been a surprise to Dr. Smith that not every dog was going to want to be petted by a stranger.

Catching Zuri's surprised face, Dr. Smith turned to her with a fake and semi-alarming grin.

"I'm sorry. She's never done that before," Zuri stammered.

"Don't worry about it," Dr. Smith's sickeningly sweet voice chimed. "Happens all the time." Finally, she left. As soon as the door closed behind her, Zuri could feel Gigi relax. She massaged Gigi's shoulders.

"It's okay, Gigi. The scary lady is gone now."

Dr. Rodriguez coughed, and Zuri remembered she wasn't alone.

"Sorry, I don't know what that was. I've never seen her bark at anyone before. She's been very chill with everyone else." She would not apologize for calling Dr. Smith scary. That was an objective truth, the same as Dr. Rodriguez being pretty.

Dr. Rodriguez looked down at Gigi, who eyed the doctor suspiciously but with no hint of aggression.

"Yes, well, you'll have to be careful when introducing her to new people. Some dogs are people, and dog selective. They get along great with some people and react poorly to others. It's just something to be mindful of so that nobody gets hurt." Dr. Rodriguez crossed the room and knelt in front of Gigi.

The Chow didn't move, and Zuri didn't feel her tense up under her fingertips, but she took hold of her harness handle again, just in case.

Dr. Rodriguez put her hand out for Gigi to sniff, but Gigi ignored it, snubbing her. Unfazed, the doctor pet the side of Gigi's face, reaching to Gigi's right and not over her head. The dog allowed it, her eyes softening.

"We didn't see any additional obstructions or find anything that looked concerning. I don't know why Gigi ate the coins, but aside from a little extra wear and tear on her digestive track, she should be okay." Dr. Rodriguez stood.

"That's a relief. I feel bad for not having the X-ray done when we were here before." Zuri sighed.

"You didn't know about the coins, and I advised you to wait. It's hard. Animals are unpredictable and unfortunately, they can't talk and tell us when something is wrong. Besides, if you had done the X-ray, Gigi would have had to go through surgery. Everything worked out in the end." The corners of Dr. Rodriguez's mouth curved up slightly. It was the closest thing to a smile that Zuri had seen cross the doctor's face.

"Wow, I thought for sure you were going to scold me for being a bad dog owner again or tell me to take Gigi back to Tails."

Dr. Rodriguez's eyes darted back to Zuri, her mouth gaping.

"I never said you were a bad dog owner," Dr. Rodriguez snapped, sounding more defensive than angry.

"You implied it. That I shouldn't have been matched with Gigi." Zuri wasn't normally the confrontational type, but she also didn't sugarcoat things or dance around them. She was direct and honest, sometimes to a fault.

"You're right, I did. I'm sorry, I was wrong."

Now Zuri was the one gaping.

"Look, we got off on the wrong foot. This is a tough job, and I see a lot of pet owners who shouldn't have animals, and even worse are the ones who don't come in when their animals are sick. You've done nothing but right by Gigi since you got her, and she clearly trusts you already. I misjudged you and I'm sorry."

Zuri opened her mouth, but she didn't know what to say. The doctor's apology seemed to be sincere and not just to placate Zuri to avoid losing her business. Before she could think of something, the vet tech came back into the room.

"Ready to go home?" the tech chimed, her smile not reaching her eyes. It was time to let the staff clock out.

"Yes." Zuri stood. Gigi followed her lead and started walking toward the door.

"Thanks again," Zuri said to her shoes as she shuffled past Dr. Rodriguez to pay their bill.

Chapter 8

Tuesday

"You're going to poke an eye out Gigi, and I really don't want to go back to the vet," Zuri scolded.

Although, if she was honest, she wouldn't mind seeing the beautiful Dr. Claudia Rodriguez again. She was a little intimidating, but she was also honest, kind, and seemed to really care about the animals she looked after. Zuri shook her head like it was an Etch A Sketch to clear the images of the doctor away. Nope. The last thing she needed was a crush on her dog's vet. That was a sure way to feed the anxiety monster living in her head every time she needed to make a vet appointment.

"Gigi." She sighed as Gigi wriggled herself farther into a bush. It already enveloped most of her body. Zuri could only see her hindquarters sticking out, tail wagging, as she undoubtedly watched a lizard that was just out of reach.

The prey drive is strong with this one, she couldn't help but think. Chasing rabbits and lizards was her favorite hobby. A couple of days ago, Zuri also learned this applied to chasing squeaky toys across the living room and in the backyard. Though Gigi never brought the toys back, her tail wagged in delight as she retrieved them. It was a side of Gigi that she hadn't seen before. Adorable.

"Seriously Gigi, let's go." Zuri lightly tugged on the leash and Gigi finally pulled herself out of the bush.

They were visiting the nearby Riparian Preserve before she got stuck at her desk, bogged down with work. The path was sometimes dirt, sometimes paved. It twisted into dense areas of shrubs and then winded away to expansive open spaces with ponds. They still had water in them now, but in the high heat of the summer, they would quickly dry up.

For Gigi, it was an endless playground with things to chase. They'd passed a few other dogs, but Gigi had only been interested in a Cattle Dog, crying after its owner pulled it away.

"Do you want some steak when we get home?" She asked. Gigi looked up at her, ears popping up.

Zuri tried to feed her gentler food that morning. Actual dog food and boiled chicken, but Gigi wasn't having it. In the eight days since she'd brought the dog home, Gigi had only eaten three times, all small amounts of steak.

She was worried Gigi was going to lose weight. Zuri put chicken broth in her water bowl, hoping it would provide some more nutrients, but that was the best she could do. She could give Gigi food, but she could not make her eat.

Although steak wasn't the best for Gigi's digestive track or her cholesterol, if she would eat it, then Zuri would feed it to her. For now, at least.

After returning from the Riparian Preserve, Gigi laid at Zuri's feet while she cooked two steaks, one for Gigi, and a breakfast steak for herself. Hash browns and a few eggs sizzled in another pan.

She plated everything, a fully loaded plate of mostly eggs with a little steak on top for Gigi, and a plate of eggs, hash browns, and steak for herself. Gigi gave her a little side eye before digging in, clearly wanting more steak on her plate, but she was finally eating a decent meal, which put Zuri at ease.

It was also nice to have someone to eat with. During her stays with her grandparents, she had eaten three meals a day at a table, but that had never really been her mom's style. Growing up, she had mostly eaten on the couch in front of the TV or in her room. This was probably the first time she had even eaten at her kitchen island table, she realized. Taking care of Gigi might help her take better care of herself.

Chapter 9

Wednesday

Four more gold coins laid in the grass before Zuri, all covered with specks of blood. Gigi whimpered and laid in the grass, her purple tongue hanging out of her mouth. It was ludicrous. Impossible.

Like breakfast the previous day, Gigi accepted leftover steak with eggs for dinner, though this time she demanded more steak be added before she would touch it.

Now, twenty-four hours after eating, she finally made to go number two, and it was gold coins again. This was crazy. Nothing had shown up on the X-ray and Zuri didn't have gold coins, or any coins at home. She was more of a card than a cash girl.

She picked up the coins with a dog poop bag and the duo slowly trudged the short distance home. They would get to the bottom of this. She wouldn't let Gigi down.

🐾 🐾 🐾

Friday

Zuri unlocked the door and let Gigi in ahead of her.

A second and then a third veterinary opinion cost her a ridiculous amount of money and Gigi an unfortunate amount of stress, all for no answers. There were no gold coins hiding in Gigi's digestive track, but there had been none on Dr. Rodriguez's tests either, and Gigi had still pooped more coins. The only explanation was that Gigi was making the coins herself, but that was impossible.

Zuri paced the living room, Gigi watching her listlessly from her memory foam bed in the corner. She needed more information. Had the previous owner known about this? Is that why they had given the dog up? Although it was difficult to imagine someone willing to give away a dog who literally pooped gold. That would be like chopping down a tree that grew money or cooking a goose that laid gold eggs.

Why hadn't she asked Julianna more questions before taking Gigi home? Gotten some history? If she went back to Tails, would Julianna give her more information? Maybe she could even contact the previous owners and ask them about it. No, she didn't want that. They might try to take Gigi back. Could they? Or would the shelter want her back? Shelters were always short on money, and they had given away a dog that pooped gold in exchange for steak.

She looked at the weary Gigi resting in the corner. If anyone had information on why this was happening and how to make it stop, she had to at least try, didn't she? For Gigi. Although the vets all assured her the dog was fine, this was not normal. Clearly, it was not fine. Even after finally eating, she had lost a couple of pounds since her vet visit with Dr. Rodriguez.

That was it. That was why Gigi didn't want to eat. She knew this would happen. Even if the coins weren't hurting her, the not eating would. If Zuri didn't make this stop, Gigi would starve herself to death.

Closing the gap between her and Gigi, she knelt to pet her. Gigi remained stoic, but Zuri could see her relaxing a little, her paws moving slightly away from her body as she allowed herself to unfurl from a tight, protective ball.

"Don't worry, Gigi. We'll figure this out," she whispered.

Chapter 10

Saturday

"Welcome to Tails Animal Shelter where—" Julianna stopped mid-sentence as recognition set in. Her eyes narrowed, and she searched around Zuri for signs she'd brought Gigi back with her.

"Don't worry, I'm not here to return Gigi." She completed the short journey from the door to the information desk. "I just have some questions. You kind of rushed me out of here the other day."

Julianna's long dark hair was pulled back into a ponytail, and it swished back and forth as she looked around. Unlike Zuri's last visit, the rude volunteer wasn't alone this time. One of the staff was cleaning the floors while another talked to potential adopters near the kennel windows.

"I'm about to go on break. Let's go talk about this somewhere quieter." She stepped around the information counter and grabbed Zuri's arm, pulling her back out the door.

"Carol!" she called to the woman by the kennels. When who Zuri assumed was Carol turned to them, Julianna yelled, "Going on break."

She pulled Zuri out the door without waiting for a response.

"Where are we going?" Zuri questioned, trying to keep up with Julianna's quick pace.

"There's a coffee shop down the street. We can talk there." Julianna continued to pull her away from the shelter. Between Julianna's quick pace and nervous glances back at the shelter, it was almost like she was running from something.

"I know how to walk without you pulling my arm," Zuri said. The words came out more annoyed than she had intended, but she was a little out of breath. It was actually supposed to be a joke, a play on a line from *Star Wars*, but Julianna didn't seem to catch the reference. She immediately stopped in her tracks and released her grip.

"Sorry!" she blurted, before continuing forward at a slower pace.

They quickly arrived at a coffee shop just down the street called Hallowed Grounds. The scent of freshly ground coffee hit them before they even opened the doors. It was obvious the building had been zoned as a home in its past life. While the outside could still be mistaken for a house, the interior was entirely cozy cafe vibes. The register and kitchen were up front near the entrance. Unlike more modern coffee shops with open layouts, Hallowed Grounds divided the seating into multiple small rooms on both the first and second floor. Some rooms had large plush armchairs and shelves of books. Others held tables and chairs, with board games stacked in the corner.

Zuri ordered a small flat white. Julianna sheepishly admitted she forgot her wallet on the rush out and Zuri ended up paying for her caramel macchiato too. They waited in silence for their drinks and then Julianna led her to a small, comfy sitting area upstairs.

The coffeehouse was mostly empty to begin with, but the second floor was deserted. Although Hallowed Grounds blasted the air conditioning, keeping the indoor temperature frigid, the second floor was still noticeably warmer. She preferred it since she hadn't brought a sweater.

"So, you're not returning Gigi, right?" Julianna's dark brown eyes searched her face intensely.

"No, no, of course not." Zuri shook her head. "You were right. We get along really well." She didn't owe the rude volunteer the reassurance, but despite Gigi's mysterious ailment, Zuri did really like the dog. Even if she had basically been forced to adopt her.

Julianna smiled smugly before sipping her coffee. Zuri inwardly rolled her eyes, a little annoyed. Julianna had nothing to be smug about. The adoption could have ended badly. What if Zuri hadn't had the money for all those tests and exams? What if she'd had to either return Gigi or put her down? What if she just hadn't liked the stubborn floof ball?

"I mean, she has cost me a lot of money, though. A few thousand dollars actually." Zuri looked at Julianna pointedly.

"I'm guessing you found out about the gold, then." Julianna leaned back in her chair.

"So, you knew about it? That she poops gold coins?" Zuri leaned forward in her seat.

"She made four coins the day she was dropped off. That was about a week before you took her home. They did some tests and found nothing. The vets assumed she must have eaten them before she was brought in and just got lucky. Then she refused to eat, so I tried feeding her some hot dogs and chicken, but she wouldn't eat any of it. I brought in some hamburgers, and she finally ate, so I brought her some more. The morning you took her, she made another four coins." Julianna pulled a coin out of her pocket.

It was the same half-dollar sized gold coin, with a wheel imprint on it that Zuri had several of at home. Four at a time.

"You should have warned me before sending her home with me. I put her through three different exams and rounds of tests for the coins alone, not even counting her initial vet visit." Zuri sighed.

"Would you have believed me?"

"Probably not. I'm still having a hard time believing it. It doesn't make sense." Zuri shook her head. Julianna shrugged.

Julianna slipped off her sneakers and pulled her feet up onto the chair, assuming a cross-legged position.

"She really was going to get euthanized if I didn't get her out of there. They weren't even going to put her on the adoption floor since she had the bald spots and wasn't eating." Julianna's eyebrows knit together in anger.

Sending a dog home with a mysterious ailment wasn't necessarily the right thing to do in Zuri's book, but she could tell Julianna really cared about all the animals. Her ethics were just questionable.

"Why didn't you take her home?" Zuri asked.

"Oh, I have cats," Julianna stated, as if this explained everything.

Usually Zuri's thoughts were written right on her face and she knew she wore her heart on her sleeve.

Today was no exception. Her brows knit together in confusion and she looked at Julianna pointedly, waiting for her to explain.

"The last time I tried to bring a dog home, it nearly killed one of my cats, so I don't bring dogs home anymore," Julianna continued.

"Not even a magical gold pooping dog?" Zuri smiled.

"Not even a gold pooping dog would make me risk my cats' lives." Julianna smiled back.

At least something finally made sense.

"Don't you get in trouble for just giving dogs away?" Zuri asked.

"No." Julianna smiled. Zuri waited, but she didn't elaborate.

"So why did the previous owner drop her off? You'd think they would want a dog who could make them rich." Zuri asked. The coins could be worthless, but they sure looked like actual gold. After getting Gigi back to eating and digesting properly, she would have them looked at, but Gigi came first.

"They passed away. It was the police who dropped Gigi off at Tails." Julianna shrugged and took another sip of her drink.

"Do you know anything else about them?" she prodded.

"Not much. Gigi belonged to an old woman. The police left her name and address but didn't have much information other than that. They found her wandering the backyard. I think they were having trouble notifying the owner's next of kin. We held Gigi for three days but no one came, so the intake staff put her on the list to be evaluated for adoption eligibility." Julianna finished her latte and set the cup down on the table between them.

"Can you get me her address? Maybe I can talk to the neighbors or see if they found her next of kin," Zuri asked.

"Why?" Julianna looked confused.

"Because Gigi is going to either starve to death or die from having her digestive track destroyed by these coins." Zuri thought that was obvious, but from the open surprise on Julianna's face, it was clear she hadn't thought things through beyond getting Gigi adopted.

"Oh. Yeah. I guess that makes sense." She nodded.

"So, will you help me? I haven't had Gigi for long, but I don't want her to die. She's important to me," Zuri stated.

"Yes! I'm always down to help an animal in need." Julianna pulled her shoes back on and stood. "I've got to get back to my post, but I'll text you what I can find in the system. We can go poke around her old address together. The police usually bring in at least one dog a day for us to hold, so if they come in today, I'll see what else I can find out from them, too."

"Great!" Zuri felt some of the tension she hadn't realized she was holding release itself from her chest.

She was relieved she no longer had to handle this by herself, and that Julianna at least had a couple of places they could start looking for answers.

Chapter 11

"Gigi, you need to go potty." Zuri tugged at the leash, but Gigi was not budging. The nearly regular monsoon rain had arrived a little early this evening, and having observed it, Gigi didn't want to go for a walk.

Julianna wasted no time texting her the information on the previous owner. There wasn't much. Astrid Drach was the woman's name. The police were asked to make a wellness call and found Astrid on the floor of her living room, already deceased. The caller had claimed to be Astrid's niece, but the police could never get back in touch with her and still hadn't found another next of kin.

She was going to meet Julianna at Astrid's house to see if they could find any clues. Since she wasn't sure how long she would be gone, she wanted to take Gigi for a quick walk. It had been a few hours since her last potty break. Although her dog pooped gold, she still peed like a regular dog.

While their back patio was covered and the dog had free range of the yard when it was cool enough outside, to her knowledge, Gigi hadn't ever gone to the bathroom back there. Laying on the dirt near the wall was her main pastime while out there. Unlike most other dogs, she seemingly didn't want to potty where she rested, even if it was outside. Zuri wasn't sure if this was another Chow Chow thing or just a Gigi thing.

Desperate times called for desperate measures. She grabbed her keys from the hook by the door. The resulting jingle grabbed the dog's full attention. Suddenly Gigi was a lot more cooperative, making her way to the car. She probably thought they were going to the Riparian Preserve, Zuri realized.

"Do you seriously think it's not raining at the park?" Zuri laughed before closing her umbrella, opening the car door, and letting Gigi into the back seat. Unfortunately, she didn't have time to take her to her favorite spot, even if it wasn't raining. They drove around to the other side of her complex instead, and Zuri parked on the street in front of a neighbor's home. Gigi got out of the car and when she realized they hadn't gone far, she looked at Zuri accusingly. Before she could get back in, Zuri closed the door and opened her umbrella.

"If you want to go home, you'd better go potty and walk fast." She smiled.

Gigi huffed in annoyance, but they quickly made their way back to their house. Despite her initial disdain for the rain, Gigi took her time in the grassy area by the pool and did her business. Relieved, Zuri got Gigi back inside and dried her off with a towel before walking back alone to get her car.

This was the most ridiculous thing Zuri had ever had to do, but if it worked, it worked.

Chapter 12

Zuri stood in front of a large, white Colonial-style house, leaning on one foot and then the other. There wasn't much chance of them getting answers here, at Astrid's home, but they had to try. Julianna was supposed to be here. She was late. A few more minutes ticked by before she finally jogged up to Zuri on the sidewalk in front of Astrid's home.

"Did you run here from the shelter?" Zuri questioned.

It would have been at least a twenty-five-minute drive, not a walkable or runnable distance, especially in this heat. Even after the brief monsoon shower, the setting sun wasted no time setting the city ablaze again. If she had said something, Zuri would have stopped to pick her up.

"No, not the shelter." Julianna heaved. "I live nearby."

A light bulb turned on in Zuri's head. If she lived in this neighborhood, or even one of the surrounding ones, it was no wonder she could spend all her time volunteering. The sprawling houses in this area were not middle-class or affordable. These were the type of barbie dream houses she used to imagine living in as a child, before she knew how much they cost.

Before she could ask any follow-up questions, Julianna strode up to the front door and began knocking. Loudly. She waited a beat and then began banging on the door even louder.

"Who do you think is in there? Didn't you say they couldn't find the next of kin?" Zuri reminded her.

Julianna continued to eye the door suspiciously before skipping back down the stairs to the sidewalk in front of Zuri.

"What are you girls doing?" A petite, older Asian woman rounded the corner with two small Yorkies. She wore a wide brimmed white hat, and a matching pink linen shirt and skirt set in a floral pattern.

"Do you know the woman who lived here?" Julianna turned to the approaching woman, smiling brilliantly.

"Astrid?" The woman raised an eyebrow. "I don't like to speak ill of the dead, but she was a mean old witch."

The woman's dogs sniffed at their feet as the woman got closer. Julianna knelt and began petting and cooing at the dogs, who seemed to appreciate her attention.

Shifting her weight from one foot to the other, arms crossed over her chest, Zuri stood awkwardly off to the side. She adored Gigi and larger dogs, but small dogs just reminded her of her mom and her impulsive tendencies. They weren't her cup of tea.

"What are you doing at Astrid's place?" the woman asked again. She seemed more curious than accusatory.

Zuri cleared her throat. "I adopted her dog. We were just wondering if any of her relatives were around to ask if they had any information about her. The dog."

"Her dog?" The woman cocked her head. "Which one?"

Zuri looked down at Julianna, a question in her eyes.

"The police only brought one dog to the shelter." Julianna stood.

"That woman was always bringing animals into that house. Animals went in and I never saw them come out." The woman shook her head.

"What else can you tell us about her?" Julianna asked.

While Zuri didn't enjoy being on the receiving end of an inquisition from Julianna, she was grateful for Julianna's skills now.

"Not much. She wasn't very social." The woman shrugged. "I have a stall at Old Gold. It's an antique store. I saw Astrid talking to the owner a few times. She might know something. Here, my card has the address on it."

She pulled a business card out of her skirt pocket and handed it to Julianna. Zuri leaned over Julianna's shoulder to read the card.

Rose Lin
Genuine Antique Jewelry
Old Gold #12
2222 S Main Street

"So you never asked her what happened to the animals?" Zuri asked softly. She looked up at Rose hesitantly.

"I did once, when I noticed her bringing in a little Yorkie, like my two here." Rose reached down to pick one dog up, holding it close to her heart. "She said they were her treasures, and they brought her wealth. Said nothing else. Never laid eyes on the little dog again."

A bunch of dogs. Never to be seen again. They brought her wealth. Zuri felt her body go rigid. Her teeth ground together as she clenched her jaw. A coincidence? She thought not.

"Well, I have to get back inside. I have to get to the gym. I'm glad one of her dogs got a nice home." She smiled at them before moving past them and down the street to the house next door, over a hundred feet away.

Julianna stood and turned to Zuri, who stared blankly at the sidewalk, hands in fists at her side.

"Let's not panic just yet. We can visit that antique store and check if the owner has any information." She pulled out her phone and did a quick google search.

"It looks like they're closed until 11 a.m. tomorrow. Let's meet there when they open?" Julianna looked up at Zuri.

"Yeah. Let's do that." She sighed. "Do you want a ride home?"

"No, it's okay. I think better when I'm moving." Julianna looked away, avoiding Zuri's gaze.

"See you tomorrow then. At eleven." She emphasized the time before walking to the driver's side of her car, which was parked on the street. Julianna waited and waved at Zuri as she pulled out onto the street before turning back down the sidewalk the way she had come.

Chapter 13

Old Gold sat in a long chain of similar, white brick buildings that ran down the length of the street. It was a mix of local and chain shops and restaurants. The walkway was covered, more to protect shoppers from the sun than for days like today with unusual daytime rain. The summer monsoon season was intent on surprising them. Climate change.

Zuri didn't like the rain, but she appreciated the cooling effect that came with it, bringing the usual triple digit heat down to the eighties. The rain would make it nice outside, if only for a few hours. She got out of her car and scrambled up to the door, flanked by two large glass display windows. The lights were off, and the doors were locked. It was 11 a.m. sharp, but there was no sign of anyone coming to open the shop. With the exception of her small sedan, the street parking in front of the shop was also empty.

The display windows held an abundance of items, from rocking chairs to knitted blankets. Jewelry shined and stuffed animals watched her with beady looking eyes. She stood waiting in front of the shop, watching as people came and went into the shops next door and across the street.

At 11:05 a.m., Zuri's phone buzzed.

Julianna: Sorry. Running Late.

At least she had texted this time. Sighing, she started typing her reply. She really didn't like it when people were late. It was so inconsiderate and rude, as if their time was more valuable than hers. In any case, there was no reason for her to come now anyway.

Zuri: They're closed. No one is here. Will have to try again later.

She hopped into her car and drove home. Gigi would be glad she was back so soon. The first time she left Gigi alone, Gigi looked up at her from in front of the door, clearly appalled that Zuri was leaving without her. Zuri hadn't known what to expect when she returned. The dog seemed to tolerate her presence, but she didn't ask for much. When she got home, Gigi greeted her enthusiastically. Or at least what counted as enthusiasm for Gigi. There was no barking or jumping. She just met Zuri at the door and wagged her tail, delighted that she had returned.

It was nice having someone to come home to, having someone happy to see her. Though it hadn't been long, she knew if Gigi was gone, her once-perfect sized house would feel empty and too big for her alone.

Another rumble from the sky sent a shiver down Zuri's spine as drops of rain beat down on her windshield.

She wouldn't let anything happen to Gigi. She turned her windshield wipers on. They were going to fix this.

The storm passed quickly. A few non-threatening but nonetheless moody clouds remained. The day was determined to be gray. She decided to take full advantage of the slightly cooler weather and brought Gigi to the Riparian Preserve. The unpaved sections of the path were a little muddy, but it was nothing they couldn't handle.

The ponds had water in them, and although their levels were still low, the water and plants helped to keep the area slightly cooler than the rest of the city as well.

Gigi was thrilled to be at her favorite place. Her tail wagged, and the leash went straight with little to no slack as she tugged, urging Zuri to walk faster.

It was really a testament to how much she already loved Gigi that she had brought her back here. Normally, walking with Gigi was very chill, even relaxing. This was the opposite. Her arm would be sore tomorrow. She had to dig her heels into the ground to keep Gigi from pulling her into a bush.

"Slow down," Zuri pleaded.

Her phone buzzed in her pocket. She pulled it out and saw a text from Julianna, asking if she wanted to go back to Old Gold.

Before she could respond, a rabbit darted in front of their path. Gigi lost her mind, pulling on the leash so hard and so fast that Zuri dropped the handle. No longer held back, the dog ran off, full speed in her pursuit.

"Gigi!" She chased after her, stuffing her phone back into her pocket.

Her hand still stung, but she needed to get Gigi back on the leash before she got lost in the bushes or the reservoirs. Although it felt secluded, there was also a busy road nearby, with only foliage to keep it fenced off.

Gigi stopped in front of a large section of bushes and bit at the branches, as if her teeth had transformed into a machete. A rabbit darted farther into the brush, causing her to lunge forward, sticking her head low as Zuri grabbed her harness.

She pulled against Zuri's hand and tried her best to follow the rabbit. Neither of them saw the small cactus hiding low to the ground until it was too late. The force of Gigi's movements drove several spikes into her face. The shock of the needles finally made Gigi lose her focus on the rabbit and she allowed Zuri to pull her back onto the path.

Although Zuri had lived in the desert her entire life, this was her first time dealing with cactus spikes. She didn't know if she should pull them out or let a veterinarian do it. With everything that had happened in the past couple of weeks, Zuri was relieved they weren't far from Dr. Rodriguez's office. They had shorter hours on Sunday, but hopefully they were still open.

Chapter 14

"We have to stop meeting like this." Dr. Rodriguez smiled at Gigi, who was laying down bravely on the exam table as the doctor removed the cactus spikes from her face. Well, sort of bravely. The corners of her mouth dipped down and her dark brown eyes looked up at Zuri pleadingly.

"Thanks for seeing us on such short notice. Again." Zuri stood on the other side of the table, doing her best to keep Gigi calm and still.

A few patients canceled because of the weather so Dr. Rodriguez could see them quickly. Although the rain had stopped earlier, it was still the sort of day that made you want to stay home. One more thing to be grateful for.

"I hope you got her insurance. If not, I strongly suggest you get some." Dr. Rodriguez said it casually, but Zuri could tell she was serious.

"I mean, I'm sure you did. Or if you didn't, that's also fine," Dr. Rodriguez added hurriedly. Her cheeks turned a rosy shade of pink and her mouth went from a small smile to a thin line.

Zuri wasn't offended this time. She knew the doctor was just looking out for her and Gigi. But even if she had been, she wouldn't blame Dr. Rodriguez for judging her this time. Losing her grip on the leash was incredibly stupid. It was an accident, but if she had been more careful, none of this would have happened.

"No, you're right, and I did get her some. Just counting our lucky stars that the waiting period finally ended." Zuri sighed. All these vet visits were making a sizable dent in her savings account. She was glad she hadn't given her mother all the money she had asked for.

Dr. Rodriguez cleared her throat. "I like your T-shirt," she said, changing the subject.

Zuri looked down to see which shirt she was wearing. Normally, she just grabbed whichever looked the most comfortable, unless she had somewhere important to be, which was rare. Today she wore a *Star Wars* T-shirt that read, *I'd Rather Kiss A Wookie.*

"Did you watch *Andor*?" she asked.

"Yeah, it was surprisingly good." Dr. Rodriguez's eyes stayed focused on the work she was doing on Gigi's face, but her lips curved up into a smile.

Before she could ask more, the beat of a very cheerful rapping on the door filled the small room. The knocker didn't wait for a response. Julianna opened the door and charged into the exam room, closing the door behind her.

"What are you doing here?" Zuri was confused. She had replied to Julianna when they got to the vet office, letting her know she had to get Gigi treated first. She had assumed that Julianna would head to Old Gold on her own.

"I was nearby at the shelter, so I thought I'd meet you here instead." Julianna shrugged before moving closer to Gigi, who didn't bark but took a step back on the table. "Hi, Gigi."

Gigi did not look interested. She looked nervously at Zuri, maybe remembering Julianna from the shelter.

"Hey, Claudia." Julianna grinned as she sat on the chair next to the door.

"Julianna," Dr. Rodriguez mumbled in greeting as she looked between her and Zuri, visibly working things out.

"Did you tell her?" Julianna leaned back in her chair.

"No, of course not," Zuri whispered. It sounded ridiculous in her head. There was no way she could say it out loud.

"It could help. We should tell her."

"Tell me what?" Dr. Rodriguez finished patching up Gigi's face and looked down at Zuri expectantly.

Zuri opened her mouth, but nothing came out. She couldn't bring herself to say it. It had been one thing to tell Julianna, who was not only already aware, but somewhat eccentric. Dr. Rodriguez would think Zuri was crazy. After visiting the other two vet offices with Gigi, she found she really liked this one. If Dr. Rodriguez didn't believe them, she would have to find a new vet. She could already see the doctor's beautiful dark eyes passing judgment on her.

"Gigi is still pooping gold and we're investigating why and how to undo it," Julianna stated plainly, as if she were just chatting about what she had for lunch or the weather.

Dr. Rodriguez looked from Julianna to Zuri and back again.

"We did testing. Gigi is fine." Dr. Rodriguez absentmindedly stroked the dog behind the ears.

"She's seen three vets, actually. The test results all showed up fine, but she's still pooping gold." Zuri pulled a small drawstring bag out of her pocket and put it on the table next to Gigi.

Dr. Rodriguez hoisted Gigi down to the floor and she shuffled away from the doctor. After giving Zuri an accusatory glance, never mind that she was the one who had run off after the rabbit, Gigi laid down at Zuri's feet, heaving a big sigh in the process. *Drama queen.*

Zuri opened the bag and dumped the coins out onto the table. She had twelve now. They all looked the same, with what looked like a dharma wheel design. She couldn't find anything like it online.

"I have eight coins too, from when Gigi was brought to the shelter." Julianna stood and walked around Gigi to the foot of the table. She pulled eight coins out of her pocket and placed them on the pile.

"The previous owner died. We went to her house to see if anyone was around, and her neighbor said she used to bring animals in, and that they never came back out," Zuri recapped, keeping her eyes on the table. She didn't want to see the disbelief she knew would be on the doctor's face.

"That's impossible. Is this one of your jokes, Julianna? It's not funny and I don't have time for this." Dr. Rodriguez crossed her hands over her chest.

"I wouldn't take Gigi to two more vets to go along with Julianna's joke." Zuri finally looked up and met the doctor's gaze. "You can call the other clinics for her records. I couldn't believe it either."

"We're going to visit an antique shop, Old Gold, where we might find some answers. Do you want to come with?" Julianna grinned.

Dr. Rodriguez's scowl intensified, but before she could answer, there was another knock at the door. Dr. Smith entered.

Gigi was immediately back on all fours, and a low growl escaped her. Zuri clipped the leash to the harness and knelt to grip the harness handle. She didn't have the spoons for another leash mishap today, especially not one that could end in a bite.

"Dr. Smith?" Dr. Rodriguez raised an eyebrow, but the other woman's gaze was transfixed on the twenty gold coins sitting on the table. She stood frozen in the doorway.

"Know something about these?" Julianna questioned, her smile falling. Zuri watched Julianna's eyes wash over the woman.

"No," Dr. Smith cleared her throat, "but I am a coin collector. I'd be happy to take them off your hands."

Julianna slid all twenty coins back into the pouch and handed it to Zuri without taking her eyes off the newcomer.

"We're not looking to sell," Julianna said.

"Did you need something, Dr. Smith?" Dr. Rodriguez asked again.

"Ah, our last couple of patients all canceled. We're going to close early." She smiled her plastic smile that made Zuri shudder.

Like the last time they had met, the woman's red ruby ring caught her eye. Light danced off the stone and Zuri couldn't seem to look away. Dr. Smith noticed and covered the ring with her other hand.

"Perfect! You can go with us," Julianna interjected, beaming at Dr. Rodriguez.

"Thanks, Dr. Smith. I'll wrap this up." She looked at the other doctor expectantly. It took several seconds before the other woman finally turned around and closed the door.

"So, that was weird," Zuri said. She spoke softly in case Dr. Smith was still near the door. "She definitely knows something about these coins."

"She sure does," Julianna agreed.

"She said she didn't." Dr. Rodriguez sighed.

They both stared at Dr. Rodriguez. *Was she serious?* This wasn't the first time Dr. Smith had barged in on Zuri's appointment and offered to take the golden coins off her hands. No one was that obsessed with coins, and even if she was, it was weird to ask for something so valuable from a customer.

"Okay, fine. It was a little weird." Dr. Rodriguez rolled her eyes.

"It's clear she's not going to tell us anything though," Julianna said.

"Obviously." Dr. Rodriguez rolled her eyes again.

"So, you believe us now, Dr. Rodriguez?"

"I guess I don't really know what to believe." She sighed.

"Gigi won't eat regularly. She's starving herself. You saw the chart. She's losing weight." Zuri let go of the harness and Gigi laid back down, her perceived threat now gone. "We need to figure this out before she gets worse."

"Help us get to the bottom of this," Julianna pleaded.

"Why do you need my help?" Dr. Rodriguez questioned.

"Because magic is obviously involved, and there's the power of three. We'll be three if you help us." Julianna flipped her long black hair over her shoulder, confident that her words made sense.

"That is the dumbest thing I've ever heard." Dr. Rodriguez grimaced.

"Don't pretend like you're not curious," Julianna said.

"Besides, you're Gigi's vet, and isn't this kind of a medical issue?" Zuri shrugged. They needed all the help they could get.

"Are you sure? My hourly for off-site visits is pretty steep." Dr. Rodriguez raised an eyebrow.

Zuri froze. Why hadn't she thought about that? She could probably figure it out depending on the rate, and the insurance might cover some of it.

"I was joking." Dr. Rodriguez sighed when she saw the look on Zuri's face. "I'm not going to charge you, relax."

Zuri felt her face get hot. Sarcasm. Right. She knew that.

"I'll meet you out front." Dr. Rodriguez went out the door that led to the back of the office.

Chapter 15

Zuri pulled up to the same strip of white buildings she'd been at earlier in the day and nabbed a parking spot right next to Dr. Rodriguez's black Honda. She had stopped at home to drop Gigi off since she doubted the store allowed pets. Gigi wasn't happy about it, but she could tell the dog was also tired. Even if Gigi were eating properly, a trip to the preserve, painful spikes to the face, and a vet visit all in one day was probably enough to make any dog need a nap.

She stepped out of her car and sprinted around to the sidewalk, appreciating the sheltered walkway for the second time that day. Dr. Rodriguez and Julianna stepped out of Dr. Rodriquez's car and joined her. Julianna was buzzing with excitement. The doctor scowled, but her face softened when her eyes met Zuri's.

"It's open!" Julianna squealed in delight as she tugged on the door handle. She rushed inside, the door swinging closed behind her. Dr. Rodriguez sighed and grabbed the flat metal handle and held the door open.

"After you."

"Thanks." Zuri walked into Old Gold and dozens of shelves immediately confronted her, all filled to the brim with antiques, most of which just looked like junk, at least to her. Her eyes scanned the room, landing on typewriters and hats. Did anyone really want an iron from the 1950s, and if so, what for?

She felt a hand wrap around her arm and looked up.

"Look, there's a cashier sign. We should start there." Dr. Rodriguez took a step down the aisle, pulling Zuri with her. Her heart danced in her chest at the contact. She knew it wasn't because she was nervous about what information the owner of Old Gold might have for them. Dr. Rodriguez let go of her arm and stopped abruptly in front of the counter. Zuri tripped over her own feet, bumping into the doctor's shoulder. Way to go.

"Sorry," she mumbled.

"Took you long enough," Julianna complained, having literally run straight to the empty counter. A bell sat next to a sign that read, *ring for assistance.* Julianna rang the bell. They waited in silence, but no one answered.

Julianna rang it again, this time repeatedly, before Dr. Rodriguez grabbed her hand to stop her.

"Enough," Dr. Rodriguez scolded before letting go of Julianna's hand and sliding the bell out of her reach.

"Can I help you?" a nasally sounding voice rang from behind them.

The trio turned around and found a slim, older Asian woman with silver hair cropped at her chin. A black beret sat on top of her head and matched perfectly with her black knitted dress and black glasses. Her dark eyes stared at them as sharply as a predator's while she took the three of them in.

"We're looking for the owner," Dr. Rodriguez stated plainly. She looked down at the woman expectantly.

"Well, you found her." The woman nodded before walking past them and around to the other side of the counter. "Violet Moody, at your service. What can I do for you?"

The three younger women turned around to continue their questioning.

"Were you a friend of Astrid Drach?" Julianna leaned on the counter, unable to contain her eagerness.

"Friend?" Violet snorted. "We are not friends. Astrid Drach is the biggest lying, thieving old crone I've ever laid eyes on. I hate that woman." She looked as if she wanted to spit.

"She passed away a couple weeks ago and my friend here," Julianna gestured to Zuri, "adopted her dog. Her dog is. . . sick, and we were hoping someone who knew Astrid might have some answers."

"The crone is dead?" Violet asked hesitantly. When Julianna nodded, a smile lit Violet's face. She danced an actual little jig while laughing. "This is the best news I've heard all month! No, all year! Haha!"

The three younger women exchanged glances. This was not the usual or most polite reaction to hearing about someone's death, even someone you hated. Astrid Drach wasn't winning any popularity contests. Out of the only two people they could find who had known her, both had referred to her as a witch, though it was possible that wasn't how Violet meant it when she called Astrid a *crone*.

"Do you know anything about these? Did Astrid maybe bring them here to sell?" Julianna looked at Zuri expectantly.

She removed the drawstring pouch from her pocket and dumped the small stack of coins onto the counter.

Violet's eyes lit up again, this time in awe. Her hands reached toward the coins, hovering over them.

"Where did you get these?" she demanded, lowering her voice. She looked around, but they were the only four in the store that Zuri could see. "Put them away. Now."

Zuri did as instructed, dumping the coins back into the bag and into her pocket.

"My dog, the one that used to belong to Astrid, she only poops these gold coins," Zuri said in a low voice, near a whisper.

She didn't know who Violet thought might overhear, but she could see how tense the woman had become. It was a good sign. She must know something. Hopefully something that could help them save Gigi.

"You shouldn't have those. They're not for the likes of you," Violet mumbled.

"So, Astrid *was* a witch!" Julianna exclaimed.

"Shhhhhh!" Violet shushed her, and at the same time, Dr. Rodriguez lightly slapped Julianna behind her head.

"Ow." Julianna rubbed the back of her head. "Was that necessary?"

"Absolutely. Calm yourself down or you'll have to wait in the car." She crossed her arms over her chest.

Zuri really wanted to know how these two knew each other. Their interactions were so intimate, but they didn't seem like friends. Not exactly.

"We're not looking for trouble," she stated quietly. "My dog is going to die if we can't reverse whatever Astrid did to make her poop the gold coins. We were hoping you could help us find some answers or point us in the right direction."

"From what Astrid's neighbor said, she must've done this to a lot of animals. They went into her house and never came out," Julianna explained, finally seeming to settle down. Maybe the slap had been exactly what she needed.

Violet's lips pursed together before they stretched into a tight line. Her eyes danced around the counter as she worked out what she wanted to say next.

"We'll give you the gold coins if you want. If you can tell us anything, anything at all," Zuri offered.

Violet's eyes shot up to meet Zuri's.

"You can't just give those away," she seethed. "You don't even realize what you have." She sighed.

"Who cares about the coins? There's a life at stake. Help us," Dr. Rodriguez chimed in.

Violet went quiet, seeming to retreat into herself once more, before she stated, "Those coins, they're worth a lot. Not in the human currency, but in the witch market."

Dr. Rodriguez put a hand over Julianna's mouth just in time to stop her squeal of excitement. She quickly removed her hand before Julianna tried to take a bite out of her fingers. The two glared at each other.

Ignoring them, Violet continued.

"They're worth about fifty thousand dollars each in witch currency. No wonder Astrid was always in here, flaunting her wealth. She always claimed it was old money. Now I know she was trading the lives of animals in exchange for gold. Black magic. Illegal animal cruelty in your world and mine."

Trading the lives of animals. That didn't sound good.

"Can we reverse it? Can we save Gigi?" Dr. Rodriguez asked, apparently ready to believe that this was real now.

Violet went quiet again, her eyes darting back and forth across the counter. Her mouth opened a few times as if she were about to say something, but she abruptly closed it again, pursing her lips. It was almost as if she was consulting with another person. Someone they couldn't see or hear.

"Maybe," she finally answered, but from the sad look in her eyes as she met Zuri's gaze, she didn't look confident.

"What do we need to do?" Zuri put her hands on the counter. The cold, smooth surface helped to ground her. She could feel a cloud of anxiety coming for her from over the horizon.

"Astrid would have had a book. A journal. A Grimoire. It's where witches document their spells, experiments, successes and failures, their history. Everything. It's all written there. If there is a way to reverse this, the only clues will be in there." Violet nodded.

"I'm guessing she would have kept that at home." Dr. Rodriguez bit her bottom lip.

"Looks like we're heading back to Astrid's." Julianna grinned excitedly. Nothing seemed to faze her.

"Bring me the Grimoire and I'll see what I can do." Violet sighed.

"Are you sure you don't want the coins?" Zuri whispered.

Violet would actually have a use for witch money, considering she was likely a witch herself. What would the three of them do with it?

"No. I won't take blood money. You keep it. Might come in handy." Violet shook her head.

Suddenly, her gaze snapped back to Zuri, an intensity radiating from her eyes.

"You're certain you've never seen these before?" the older woman asked, pointing to the coins in Zuri's pocket.

"Never." Zuri looked away, feeling a bit uncomfortable under the witch's gaze.

The woman hummed and continued her assessment of Zuri until the door opened and another customer came charging toward the desk, in need of Violet's help. The three women shuffled out of the store before the witch could change her mind about helping them.

"Do you think she has a familiar?" Julianna asked when they were back outside the shop. She turned toward the door, but before she could take a step to go back inside, Dr. Rodrigez grabbed the back of her shirt, yanking her backward.

"Focus, Julianna. We need to get that book." Dr. Rodriguez scowled.

"So you believe us now? That my dog is enchanted?" She shifted her weight back and forth between her right and left feet.

"I don't understand how any of this could be real." Dr. Rodriguez sighed.

It wasn't an, *I believe you*, but it was enough for Zuri. At least she wouldn't have to find a new vet.

"The storm seems to have passed. Let's go to Astrid's!" Julianna jumped up and down in anticipation.

"We should probably wait until after dark," Zuri said. It was still early, and the sun wouldn't set for another few hours. They shouldn't be caught snooping around someone else's property.

"Good idea! I'll go get us some latex gloves." Julianna beamed.

Zuri and Dr. Rodriguez blinked at her blankly.

"So we don't leave fingerprints." Julianna turned to walk off.

"See you at ten." She waved.

Chapter 16

Three women of color breaking and entering in a very wealthy and very white neighborhood. What could possibly go wrong, Zuri wanted to say, but she sighed instead.

It wasn't like they had any better options. They had already tried to get into Astrid's house the legal way, but no one was home and the next of kin were nowhere to be found.

It was dark now. They had all gone home from Old Gold separately and changed into black clothing. Zuri checked on Gigi, who seemed to be feeling better, good enough to eat some steak over rice. She felt bad feeding her, knowing the painful outcome, but she couldn't live off water forever.

A few hours later, Dr. Rodriguez picked Zuri up with Julianna already in the car. Astrid's house backed up against a canal and green belt. Instead of parking in front of the home, Julianna had Dr. Rodriguez park at a trail entrance almost a mile away. Although Julianna still wouldn't be specific, at least not in front of Zuri, it was obvious she was familiar with Astrid's general neighborhood. She hadn't been joking about the gloves either. She gave them each a pair to put in their pockets until they got to the house and led them down the trail where they could enter Astrid's property from the backyard.

The path wasn't lit, and signs showed the trail was closed from sundown to sunup. The storm had passed, but soft clouds remained, obscuring the moon and any visible stars. It was dark and the ominous noises from the canal and the nearby bushes weren't helping to make things any less creepy.

"You alright?" Dr. Rodriguez whispered, breaking the near quiet and making Zuri jump. She heard Julianna snort a laugh from a few feet ahead of them.

"Yeah, I'm fine." She cleared her throat.

"Not scared of the dark, are you?" She could hear a smile in Dr. Rodriguez's voice.

"Of course not." Zuri felt herself smile too, despite her reservations about this entire mission.

Julianna, ever the energizer bunny, kept getting farther and farther ahead of them, unable to contain her excitement.

"Don't worry, if anyone comes after us, I can take 'em." Dr. Rodriguez made a fist with her right hand

and Zuri heard the slap as she punched into her left palm.

"Is that right?" She laughed.

"I go to a boxing gym a few times a week."

"Is that how you paid for vet school? Underground fight club?" Zuri surprised herself by asking.

The doctor snorted a laugh, and it was music to her ears.

"It helps me unwind." She rolled her shoulders back. "A lot of people don't know this, but veterinarians have high rates of depression and even suicide. Getting to punch things, and sometimes people, helps."

"That makes sense," Zuri said. She always thought veterinarians must be living the dream, getting to help animals every day, but now that she thought about it, it must be stressful. She wondered how much of the job was wellness checks with healthy dogs versus treating sick animals, or worse, having to euthanize them.

"So, Julianna," Dr. Rodriguez started, slowing her steps so she was right next to Zuri. "She's just helping you with Gigi, right? You're not. . ." She trailed off, but Zuri had no idea where she was going with her question.

"Not what?"

Dr. Rodriguez cleared her throat. "Not dating or anything?"

Her eyes widened in surprise. What would have possibly led the doctor to think that? If anyone looked like they were dating, it was—

Oh.

Was Dr. Rodriguez interested in Julianna? Or had they already dated, and she wanted to get back together? Julianna *was* pretty. She was also confident and read people like they were books. Although she was a few inches shorter than Zuri, her confidence always made her seem taller.

"No, no. Nothing like that." She waved her hands in emphasis.

Dr. Rodriguez said nothing in response, and Zuri was too nervous to look over at her to see her facial expression.

"Did you and Julianna date?" Zuri asked.

Dr. Rodriguez stopped in her tracks.

"No! Never." She shuddered in disgust before beginning to walk again, easily catching up to Zuri. "Why would you think that?"

"You just seemed close. Sorry, I shouldn't have asked or assumed you were even interested in women." She bit her cheek and wished she had something to do with her hands. Why did she have to make things awkward?

"She used to date my younger sister. It was a while ago. It lasted about a year but was nothing serious for either of them, apparently. We also run into each other a lot with my work and her volunteering." Dr. Rodriguez scrunched up her face again, as if just the thought of dating Julianna made her sick.

Zuri felt a weight lift off her chest.

"For the record, you're not my type either, Claudia," Julianna chimed in.

They both startled in surprise. Neither of them had noticed that she had come back to them. It was so dark they hadn't seen her.

"I can see why you might think I was dating Zuri, though. She's kind of a catch. She has a good job, she owns her townhome, and you have to admit, she's pretty cute." Julianna said as she walked backward and winked at Zuri. Actually winked. First of all, who did that anymore? Second, it was unfair that Julianna could pull it off.

Zuri felt her cheeks flush. Now Dr. Rodriguez was going to think Julianna thought that she was interested in her, which wasn't possible. She needed to have a talk with Julianna. This was not the place or time to be trying to be her wing woman. For now, she would have to change the subject.

"When are you going to tell me why you can volunteer all the time instead of working? And which one of these rich people's houses is yours?" Zuri changed the subject.

"Who said I don't work?" Julianna grinned as she walked away, not answering the question. Zuri and Dr. Rodriguez followed behind her.

"Why are you so vague? Can't you just be straight with me?" Zuri sighed.

"I've never been straight so, don't think so," Julianna threw over her shoulder.

"You know that's not what I meant." Zuri groaned.

"We're here." Julianna turned and walked off the path, into the canal. It was mostly empty except for a few puddles from the earlier rain. She walked down it and used the rocks and small shrubs as hand and footholds to climb up the other side.

Dr. Rodriguez and Zuri followed her lead. Zuri was not happy about how dirty her hands and clothes were getting, but it was for Gigi.

On the other side of the canal, there was a six-foot brick wall that had to be scaled. Julianna put on her gloves and clasped her hands together, making a foothold. Dr. Rodriguez stepped into her hands without hesitation and reached for the edge of the wall as Julianna boosted her up. She pulled herself up and straddled the wall.

"You next," Julianna commanded.

Zuri stepped into Julianna's hands, and like Dr. Rodriguez, pulled herself on top of the wall, just barely. The effort caused her heart to pound, and it took her a solid minute to catch her breath. She really needed to start working out.

Julianna took a couple steps back from the wall, and with a running start, jumped up and grabbed the edge, easily pulling herself up. It almost seemed practiced, like she'd done this sort of thing before. Maybe she had. Her secret job could be anything, a spy or even a secret agent.

"Put on your gloves!" Julianna whispered sharply.

Zuri and Dr. Rodriguez did as instructed, and the three of them jumped down.

Zuri looked around. The yard was full of weeds and the tall grass had turned yellow. The large white house ahead was pitch black, with no signs of life. Although the neighboring houses weren't right next to each other, someone might still see them walking through the yard if they happened to look out from their second-story window, even with the cover of night. So, they stayed along the wall, crouched low.

They made their way to the back of the house and found the patio's sliding door. Julianna tugged on the handle, and it easily slid open. With the owner and sole occupant deceased and no next of kin to care for the property, no one had bothered to make sure it was locked up.

Julianna turned and grinned at Dr. Rodriguez and Zuri. Dr. Rodriguez's lips pressed together and she rolled her eyes, but Zuri saw a slight uptick in the corners of her mouth. Zuri looked around the door but didn't see any obvious motion detectors. No alarms sounded, and no lights turned on. Julianna took a careful step inside and turned on her cell phone's flashlight.

The light swept the room, illuminating furniture and generic wall art, the kind you might see in a model unit. The layout was open and from the back door, they could see a dining room, large living room, and a large kitchen. Everything was spotless and a little sterile looking. There wasn't much personality or any sign that someone actually lived there. No sweater hung off the back of a couch. No books left out. Not even a single dish rested in the sink.

Walking farther into the house, near the front door, the trio glanced at the stairs. There was a door underneath the stairs, just a closet probably, but Zuri felt her hand reach for the knob, instinctively. Something was calling for her attention. It was like that nagging feeling she sometimes got in the back of her mind when she was leaving the house, knowing that she had forgotten something, and then realized she didn't have her wallet. Or when she thought about needing to call someone and moments later, her phone rang. She needed to open the door, so she did.

Julianna shined her light through the open doorway, revealing a set of stairs that led down beneath the house. Not a closet. A basement. Weird.

Zuri knew from her home search a few years ago that it was rare for a house in Arizona to have a basement.The ground was too hard, making the cost of adding one unpredictable and unappealing. You could occasionally find a house with one, but it wasn't common.

"Why don't you two look for the Grimoire down there, and I'll look for more clues upstairs," Julianna suggested.

"Why do we have to go down in the creepy basement while you get to stay up here?" Zuri argued.

"We can't split up." Dr. Rodriguez huffed. "We're not white people in a horror movie."

Zuri snorted a laugh.

"We're not in a horror movie, so it'll be fine." Julianna shrugged before trotting up the stairs, refusing to debate it any further. The light faded as she reached the top of the stairs, leaving Dr. Rodriguez and Zuri in the dark.

Dr. Rodriguez pulled up her phone's flashlight and Zuri followed suit. Once they were downstairs, there was no chance of someone seeing the lights through the windows, anyway.

Zuri took a step toward the door, but she stopped and nearly jumped when she felt a hand grab hers. Maybe she was more scared than she cared to admit. She turned to look back. It was just Dr. Rodriguez.

"Are you scared?" Zuri whispered as she tried to ignore the warm heat of Dr. Rodriguez's hand in hers. Her hand was probably clammy and cold in comparison, but if the doctor minded, she didn't mind enough to let go.

"No, but we're about to walk into a witch's basement. Julianna might be dumb enough to go off on her own, but I'm not taking any chances on us getting separated down there." Dr. Rodriguez gripped Zuri's hand a little tighter.

Zuri nodded and stepped through the door and onto the staircase, the doctor right behind her. She couldn't hold her phone, Dr. Rodriguez's hand, and grab the stair railing, so she took each step carefully, one at a time. A few steps down, they heard a low screech and a click as the door closed on its own.

"Nope." She heard Dr. Rodriguez whisper. Despite the creepiness of the situation, a laugh escaped her. She felt Dr. Rodriguez squeeze her hand again before loosening her grip a little.

At the bottom of the stairs, they both flashed their lights around the room.

The walls were jagged and made of some kind of crystal or sparkling rock that seamlessly went from wall to ceiling. A large black cauldron filled the center of the room, drawing their eyes. A long desk stood close to the wall to their left, with enough space to walk around it. The top of the desk was covered with all kinds of vials, note pages, flowers, and bottles. The floor was littered with crumpled up paper, dirty dishes, and rotting food. It was hard to breathe, the odor of decay making her want to vomit.

Zuri's jaw dropped when her eyes landed on a pile of animal bones to their right.

"Dr. Rodriguez, look," she whispered, gesturing to the pile with her phone light. There had to be tens of skulls, rib cages, and paws piled high. Bodies of all sizes picked clean of flesh. She took a small step back, bumping into Dr. Rodriguez, who stood slightly behind her.

"You can call me Claudia." She felt the doctor's warm breath brush her ear.

"Okay," she mumbled, feeling blood rush to her cheeks.

"Let's look for the magic book," Claudia whispered as she stepped to the left, her right hand still holding Zuri's firmly. She tugged Zuri along behind her.

Zuri put her phone in her pocket when they reached the desk. While Claudia illuminated the desk's contents with her phone, Zuri picked up and moved items, hoping they would know what they were looking for when they saw it.

The book had to be big, in theory, but it was also a magic book. It could probably be any size and still hold an infinite number of pages or information, like Mary Poppins's bag, for all they knew. Nothing obvious stuck out.

Claudia slowly roamed the room with her phone light once more, this time illuminating an alcove under the stairs that they hadn't seen when standing at the landing. From where they stood, especially in the dark, it was impossible to see what the alcove was hiding. A monster could be lurking in the shadows, and they wouldn't be able to see it until it was too late.

"We should go look in the dark creepy alcove, shouldn't we?" she whispered.

"Unfortunately." Claudia nodded.

"I can go alone, and you can wait by the stairs," Zuri offered, but she really hoped Claudia would go with her.

"We're not splitting up." Claudia squeezed her hand, and they began the short trek to the other side of the room.

Instead of a closet or an additional staircase, the area was open, but the wall was still made of the same crystal-like rocks. There was a small, half-circle shaped cutout shelf in the wall, with a few candles and dead flowers on either end, and a big, black book that sat in the center.

Zuri reached out with her free hand, but before she reached the book, it floated off the shelf and moved to levitate in front of her. She felt Claudia jump backward, her hand pulling Zuri along with her. The book moved forward a few inches, following.

"That's a big book. I might need my hand back." She looked at Claudia as she tried unsuccessfully to release it from her grip.

Claudia slowly let go and grabbed onto her shirt instead, determined they stayed together, no matter what.

Zuri reached out and picked up the book. As soon as her hands gripped it, whatever magic that had held it weightless in the air ceased and she felt its mass in her arms. This was the book. It had to be. There was nothing else there that remotely looked important enough to be a Grimoire.

Carefully, she held it up, Claudia kindly providing her with some light. *Grimoire of Astrid Drach*, was the single line in the center of the cover, written in gold.

"This is it. Let's get out of here." Zuri stepped backward into Claudia again. She really needed to watch where she was going.

"Sorry," she whispered, stepping to the side.

"Don't worry about it," Claudia answered.

They slowly made their way back up the stairs. Zuri cradled the book against her chest with one hand and held onto the stair rail with the other. Claudia shined the phone's flashlight in front of them, but still clung to the back of Zuri's shirt with her free hand. When they reached the landing at the top of the stairs, the door was gone.

"Houston, we have a problem," she whispered.

Claudia's phone light traced the wall where the door should have been. It was just the same solid crystal stone as the rest of the basement now. She stepped next to Zuri, letting go of her shirt, and felt the wall.

They both jumped, nearly falling down the stairs, when Zuri's phone rang. The name *Julianna*, illuminated the black screen.

"Where are you two?" Julianna hissed, her voice uncharacteristically angry sounding. Zuri heard a doorknob jangle in the background.

"We're stuck. The door disappeared. Is it still there on your side?" Zuri asked.

"Yes, but it won't open." Julianna grunted. It sounded like she was fighting with the door and the door was winning.

"It's a magic basement. Maybe we need to say the magic word?" Claudia said.

"Abracadabra," Zuri tried. Nothing.

"Open Pocus!" Claudia cried. Nothing.

"Open Sesame." Zuri shrugged. No door.

"Did you find the Grimoire?" Julianna asked.

"Yeah," Zuri answered, pulling the book from under her arm and holding it with her free hand in front of her. She had to keep it wedged against her stomach or she'd drop it. It was heavy.

"Maybe you should try seeing if there's anything in the book," Julianna suggested.

Zuri handed Claudia her phone and held the book with both of her hands. *Zap.* A shock ran through her fingertips, traveling through her entire body, causing her to drop the book.

"What happened?" She heard Julianna's voice through the phone.

"I think the book electrocuted me. A warning shock maybe?" Zuri stooped down in front of the book. She didn't want to touch it again, but Gigi was counting on them bringing this book back to Violet. If there was any hope of saving Gigi, it was in the book. She poked it and when it didn't zap her again, picked it back up and stood.

Crunch. A noise came from below them in the basement.

They weren't alone. Zuri felt her heart trying to explode out of her chest. She'd managed to be brave this long, numbing herself to her fear, but she couldn't hold back the panic welling up inside her much longer.

She needed to get a grip. She closed her eyes and took a deep breath.

Please, just open. Come back door. She wished with all her might that they could somehow get out of there.

Crunch. Whatever was down there was moving closer. *Please, open.*

Before she could open her eyes, she heard the eerie whine of the door opening and felt Claudia yanking her through. When she opened her eyes again, they were out of the basement. Julianna slammed the door closed behind them. Without looking back, Claudia pulled at Zuri's arm, leading her to the back door. They had the book. It was time to go.

Chapter 17

Claudia pulled up to the curb across from Zuri's house where a black sedan that was still running blocked the driveway. A tall white man with brown hair peeked into Zuri's windows. He wore a khaki uniform of some kind, but from the distance of the walkway, Zuri couldn't make out what kind.

"Do you know that guy?" Claudia raised an eyebrow, putting the car in park.

"No, but there's been a lot of break-ins in my neighborhood lately." She pulled out her phone and began filming the man, who hadn't seemed to notice them parked across the street.

Claudia pulled out her phone too and opened the dial pad, but Zuri grabbed her wrist before she could dial. "I'm not sure we should call the police yet. You know, since we just broke into a house. Let's see what he's up to first."

"What are you doing?" Julianna yelled to the man as she opened the car door and started walking toward him.

He jumped before turning to face her.

Zuri let go of Claudia's wrist and hopped out of the car, rushing around it to stand next to Julianna, who had paused in the middle of the street. Was this girl crazy? Apparently, she hadn't considered the possibility that the man could be armed.

She heard a car door shut and felt Claudia's presence beside her. Together, they approached the man, making the short journey across the street. She noticed the quality of his uniform was poor. The fabric, thin and cheap, resembled a costume. There was a badge that said, "Animal Control," on the right side of his chest, but no city or county name and no officer name either.

"Animal Control," the man stated, crossing his arms over his chest.

"And you're trying to break into our friend's house because. . .?" Claudia mirrored his stance as best as she could, tucking the Grimoire under her arm.

"I got a report about a dog being abused at this address." He looked at them pointedly.

"From who?" Julianna questioned, her voice entirely disbelieving.

"Anonymous," the man answered without missing a beat, tilting his chin up.

"I'm her veterinarian and she's from the animal rescue where the dog came from. Whatever call you got was bogus." Claudia glared at him.

"I'm going to need to take the dog with me. To be examined." He stepped closer.

"You're not taking my dog anywhere. You have an unmarked car, haven't shown us any ID, and tried to break into my house. I'm calling the police," Zuri said.

She pulled her phone out of her pocket and began to dial. She didn't want to talk to the police after just having stolen something herself, but she'd do anything for Gigi. Before she could hit the call button, the man bolted back to the SUV and sped down the street, but not before Julianna could take a few pictures of his license plate.

"Well, that was something," Claudia murmured.

"Seriously!" Julianna nearly shouted. "What are the odds that we would come back from breaking into a house and find someone trying to break into yours?"

"Please say that again, a little louder. I don't think *all* of my neighbors heard you." Zuri sighed, marching up to the front door. Hopefully nosy Donna hadn't been watching. She glanced toward her neighbor's living room windows but didn't see any movement at the curtains. That was a relief.

"Do you want us to stay with you?" Julianna followed her.

She didn't want to be alone, but she didn't want to inconvenience them. They had done enough already, helping her break into a witch's house for the Grimoire. Claudia probably had to work the next day and Julianna would need to. . . volunteer or do whatever it was that Julianna did for a living.

"No, it's okay. I'll be alright." She put her key into the lock and turned it.

"We're staying." Claudia reached past her, opening the door.

They both pushed past her, letting themselves into Zuri's home. She followed, feeling reluctant and relieved at the same time.

"And in the morning, I'm making waffles!" Julianna yelled.

"Calm down, she's got neighbors." Claudia tried to smack the back of Julianna's head, but she dodged, pulling to the side and out of reach.

Gigi greeted Zuri at the door, tail wagging, and blatantly ignored their guests. Zuri locked the door behind them before stooping down to pet Gigi, running her hands through her soft black fur.

"Make yourselves at home." She looked and saw Julianna doing exactly that. Her long hair trailed behind her as she rushed around the living room, picking things up and not exactly putting them back where they belonged. Meanwhile, Claudia left the Grimoire on the coffee table and was checking the lock on Zuri's sliding door that led out to the small backyard and patio.

"You know they sell locks that go up at the top of these doors. We'll need to pick one up tomorrow."

Claudia turned around to see Zuri's hands engulfed in the fluffy fur of Gigi's rear end as she whisper-sang, "wiggle wiggle wiggle wiggle wiggle" in a high-pitched voice. Gigi loved butt rubs. Zuri was also sure she liked her singing, despite never saying so.

"That's a good idea." She cleared her throat and stood. Her cheeks were warm after being caught doing something so silly.

"Um, I need to walk Gigi real quick."

"Normally, I'd be all for a walk, but after that man just tried to take her, maybe she should just use the backyard," Julianna said, rejoining them in the living room after perusing Zuri's bedroom.

"I don't think she's ever peed out there. She's *really* particular about where she goes to the bathroom." She reached for Gigi's leash off the hook on the wall.

"Claudia, go with her and I'll stay here and make sure no one else tries to break in," Julianna suggested as she began looking through Zuri's bookshelf.

If Zuri had known someone was going to go through it, she might have hidden a few of the books on the shelf, but she so rarely had anyone over. There were a few romance books she had absolutely not read for the plot or great writing, and she knew without a doubt Julianna would find those exact books on the shelf. Hopefully, she wouldn't use what she found as ammunition later.

Claudia rolled her eyes at Julianna, who looked anything but alert, but she didn't argue. They left her townhouse and walked in a mostly comfortable silence, taking the usual route through the neighborhood. Gigi led the way. Claudia walked with her arms crossed over her chest, eyes scanning every car, shadow, and doorway.

"Thanks for all your help," Zuri started, breaking the silence. "I'm not sure I would have broken into a witch's house for an acquaintance."

"Acquaintance?" She saw a smile tug at Claudia's lips and felt her own turn up in response. "We have the shared trauma of escaping a witch's basement together. I think that elevates us to friends automatically."

Claudia laughed, and her arms dropped to her sides. She stopped scanning their surroundings, letting her dark eyes meet Zuri's.

"Why *are* you doing this?" She couldn't help but ask.

Julianna was the one who had given her Gigi, to try and save her from getting euthanized. She had basically stolen the dog from the shelter, so it made sense that she would do anything to help. Claudia though? What was she getting out of this? She was still trying to figure it out.

Claudia sighed and ran a hand through her dark hair before she answered. Zuri saw her shoulders tensing up.

"My cat, Charlotte, died not too long ago. Okay, it was more like a year ago, but I'm still devastated. If I can help someone else keep their pet alive, I just feel like I have to. For Charlotte."

Claudia resumed scanning their surroundings and avoided eye contact.

"What happened to Charlotte?" Zuri asked quietly. She wasn't sure if she should ask or not, but her curiosity got the better of her.

"She got sick." Claudia dropped her gaze to the road. "It was sudden, and I tried really hard to save her, but in the end, there was nothing I could do. I had to let her go."

Zuri didn't know what to say. Neither words nor people were really her thing. Finding something comforting to say in this situation just didn't come naturally to her. In the end, she couldn't think of anything to say about Charlotte. Instead, she said, "Thank you, for helping save Gigi."

🐾 🐾 🐾

The trio huddled around the Grimoire, which sat between them on the coffee table. The book was strange. Both Claudia and Julianna had tried to open it while Zuri took a shower, but it refused to open. The cover remained closed, as if all the pages were glued together. It was only when Zuri reached for it that the book flew open of its own accord, her hand hovering a few inches away.

Both Claudia and Julianna leaned in close, but Zuri struggled to focus with Claudia's thigh pressed against hers. She smelled faintly of roses, despite all the walking and running around they had done earlier in the night.

Zuri lent them both some pajamas, broke out some snacks, and shared her favorite spicy herbal chai tea. They flipped through the book for over an hour and found nothing useful. There were spells for anything and everything, from cleaning a toilet to fixing a broken phone screen. Nothing so far about making animals poop gold.

"It's getting late." Claudia yawned. "We should get some sleep."

"I have extra toothbrushes under the bathroom sink," Zuri said, shutting the Grimoire.

Without hesitation, Claudia stood and made her way to the bathroom. Zuri's eyes followed her until she was out of sight, down the short hallway. She turned back and nearly jumped when her eyes met Julianna's, a smug grin on her face.

"You like her," she whispered, surprisingly tactful for once.

"I don't even know her," Zuri whispered back. "And don't say things like that. I don't want her to feel uncomfortable staying the night."

"You can be attracted to someone without knowing them well." Julianna snorted. "Anyway, if it's really supposed to be a secret, you should probably learn how to hide it better. It's written all over your face." Julianna stood and made her way to the bathroom. She heard the two bickering as they fought for space at the sink.

It had been a long time since she'd dated anyone, not that she had much experience to begin with. Just a few women in college. She wasn't the casual hook-up type, but her relationships had all been short, lasting only a few weeks or months.

She struggled to let people in, and in the age of instant gratification, it wasn't easy to find someone who was patient. Not that it mattered. She was doing just fine on her own. She didn't need to be like her mother, jumping in and out of toxic relationships and losing herself. This independence that she had spent years building for herself, that was what she needed. She wouldn't let this small crush ruin everything.

Zuri picked up the Grimoire and looked around. She couldn't just leave it on the table. The book was too important to risk it going missing, especially after that weird encounter with the likely fake animal control officer.

She stood and took the book into the kitchen, tucking it way back into a cabinet with her mixing bowls and baking pans. It should feel at home there. Baking was kind of like magic.

Next, she went to her coat closet and grabbed a lightweight silver baseball bat she had bought years ago for a Halloween costume. There had been a time when she had kept it in her bedroom to make her feel safer. Then she had worried if she would even be able to use it on someone or if they would end up hitting her with it instead. What if she accidentally hit them too hard and killed them? The bat had been cheap and made for children, so it wasn't that heavy, but still. Her anxiety battled over the pros and cons of using it to protect herself and hurting someone else in a way that might result in permanent consequences. It was stupid, but the latter had won, leading the bat to sitting unused and nearly forgotten about in a closet. Now she tucked it next to the nightstand in her bedroom. She wouldn't hit someone with it for her own sake, but maybe for Gigi's.

Satisfied, Zuri went to the bathroom as her two guests bickered their way to the kitchen to grab some water. She brushed her teeth, trying not to dwell on what Julianna said. She just had a teensy tiny crush. That was it. It would go away on its own. She just needed to get out more. This was the first time since she'd bought her current house that she'd even had anyone besides a repair person over.

Teeth brushed and face washed, she headed into her bedroom. Luckily, she had lots of blankets. The real problem was, where were they going to sleep? She didn't have a guest bed, just the couch, and it wouldn't fit both of them.

She grabbed the extra blankets from her closet, but before she could do anything with them, Julianna waltzed in and grabbed the stack.

"You don't snore, do you?" Julianna tossed the stack on the bed and started pulling the covers down.

"What are you doing?" Zuri closed the closet.

"We just stole a witch's Grimoire and stopped someone from trying to steal Gigi."

That still didn't answer her question. She stared at Julianna pointedly.

"Your bed is enormous. We can all fit." Julianna climbed in, cocooning herself in a blanket.

It was true. She had a king and none of them were that large.

"Is that okay with you?" Claudia stood in the doorway, giving Julianna a disapproving look.

Zuri looked at Claudia. "Yeah, it's fine."

She shrugged and turned to meet Zuri's eyes. "There's still the couch. Just, you know, as an option."

"It's fine." She looked at the floor. So many thoughts swirled in her mind it was hard to tell one apart from the other. She was used to having her own space. It had been years since she had ever had a sleepover. They barely knew each other, but they were staying the night at her house. What if she talked in her sleep? She might say something embarrassing. Would they think she was weird if she did sleep on the couch? Would they be offended?

"I'll probably have nightmares about that basement" Claudia shook her head, her eyes glazed over. Zuri recalled the pile of bones and the smell of decay. Something had been down there with them. If, by chance, it had followed them back to her place, she didn't want it to find her alone on the couch. The thought spiral in her head eased. For once, having other people around brought her some relief.

Sleeping arrangements apparently decided, Zuri took Gigi out front for one last potty break in the grass, right outside the pool area across from her driveway. Claudia watched from the door.

They climbed into Zuri's bed with Julianna already fast asleep. Zuri laid in the middle, Julianna and Claudia to her left and right. From her bed, Gigi gave her a dirty look as if to say, *they better not disturb my beauty sleep*, before closing her eyes and burrowing into a little dog donut.

Chapter 18

The thump of hard footsteps stirred Zuri out of her sleep. She felt something heavy across her side. Opening her eyes, she found herself face to face with a sleeping Julianna. Her mouth hung open and a puddle of drool marked her pillow. Zuri moved away, taking back a few inches of space, but not quite escaping the weight of Julianna's limbs.

Stomp.

Someone was in the living room. Claudia? Maybe she really couldn't sleep after the basement incident. Zuri turned over, pulling away from the arm and leg Julianna had draped over her, but instead of empty space, Claudia lay there, sleeping as soundly as Julianna.

A low growl from Gigi kicked Zuri into action. Jumping out of bed, she quickly grabbed the silver bat and positioned herself behind the bedroom door. She didn't care about her stuff in the living room. Everything important was in the bedroom with her, Gigi and her new friends.

Gigi stood and stalked toward the closed bedroom door, sniffing at the doorframe. The knob quietly turned. Gigi barked as the intruder opened the door. As soon as they saw the dog, they lunged toward her without hesitation.

Zuri slammed the door into the intruder, who hadn't yet cleared the doorway.

They shouted in pain, and more voices joined as Julianna and Claudia were woken by the commotion.

She stepped out from behind the door as the intruder recovered. They swung the door open, and she met them with her bat, swinging, hitting the intruder's torso multiple times. The intruder retreated through the living room's sliding door. She followed, swinging the bat and hitting them as hard as she could until they cleared the wall.

Someone grabbed her shirt from behind. She swung the bat, stopping just in time. Claudia. The bat stopped an inch from her face. She had almost bashed Claudia's face in.

"Get back inside! Now," Claudia demanded, turning toward the house. She pulled on Zuri's shirt until they passed through the door. After sliding it shut, Claudia drew the curtains closed for good measure.

"Is everyone okay?" Julianna asked.

Zuri nodded. Her gaze focused on Gigi, who peeked her head through the curtain of the sliding door. Her tail swayed a few times as she gazed into the backyard.

"That was the same man from earlier," Claudia stated definitively, crossing her arms over her chest.

"I didn't get a good look at him. Are you sure?" Zuri moved away from the sliding door and sat on the couch, finally dropping the bat. She was so focused on hitting the intruder, she hadn't taken the time to register what they looked like. It was all kind of a blur. Her hands shook, and she shoved them beneath her, hoping no one had noticed.

"Positive." Claudia nodded. "He wasn't wearing a mask. Same build, face, and hair."

"Who do you think he is?" Zuri asked no one in particular.

"Violet said these coins were worth a lot of money. It must be someone who knows about Gigi and wants the coins. Let's make a list. Who knows about Gigi and the coins?" Claudia moved to sit down in front of the coffee table. She pulled out her phone and opened her notes app.

"The three of us, Violet, and I guess any of the vet offices you went to, Zuri," Julianna listed off before flopping down on the other side of the couch.

"Neither of you told anyone?" Zuri questioned. There had been little time for Claudia to tell anyone, but Julianna might have. She wouldn't have blamed them if they had. She mostly questioned if the other person would have believed them. A gold pooping dog sounds as ridiculous as actual money growing on trees.

They both shook their heads.

"Which other vet offices did you visit?" Claudia frowned, annoyance written all over her face. Zuri could practically see the thought bubble appear over Claudia's head. *How dare she have gone to another clinic. How dare Zuri second-guess her opinion of Gigi's health.* She grinned and held back a laugh before listing off the other offices.

"The only person interested in the coins was the other vet at your office. Remember? She was really weird about it," Zuri reminded them.

The doctor had barged into their appointment with Claudia twice to inquire about Gigi and the coins.

"Dr. Rachel Smith." Claudia noted in her app.

"What if she heard us talking about going to Old Gold after leaving the clinic? She would have known that I might not be home, that Gigi might be alone." Her eyebrows knit together. Her smile faded.

"What do you know about her?" Julianna made herself more comfortable on the couch, extending her legs and feet toward Zuri, though her feet didn't quite reach her. Like her bed, she had opted for a large and comfortable couch. Both were a bit excessive for a single person, but she needed soft places to retreat into her blanket caves at the end of the day.

"Not much. She hasn't been working at the clinic long. I don't like to get too friendly with the other staff. Boundaries, you know?" Claudia shrugged.

Julianna laughed.

"Don't start, Julianna," Claudia warned.

Claudia turned to glare at her. Zuri looked between them.

"You're at a client's house now. And was Elizabeth not on staff?" Julianna said, ignoring Claudia.

"Who's Elizabeth?" Zuri asked.

"Claudia's ex-girlfriend, who was not only staff at the same clinic, but Claudia's subordinate," Julianna revealed.

Zuri couldn't keep her jaw from dropping. Her eyes darted to Claudia, who looked like she might leap over the coffee table and smother Julianna with a pillow.

"That was a long time ago. I was young and stupid. I won't make that mistake again. And this is different. This is an emergency. A magical emergency."

"So, what happened?" She tried to ask casually, but she was interested. She couldn't imagine Claudia doing something as scandalous as dating a subordinate. But then again, she'd just broken into a house with Zuri. She didn't really know her that well.

"Shouldn't we focus on figuring out who tried to kidnap Gigi?" Claudia questioned.

"Right." She tried to refocus. Priorities. "Are we sure they were trying to get Gigi? My neighborhood has had a lot of robberies in the last few weeks."

"It was definitely the same fake animal control officer, so yes, this was no normal robbery," Claudia stated.

"Plus, why wake us up by coming into the bedroom? A normal robber would just start grabbing the most valuable things and book it," Julianna agreed.

"Just trying to cover all explanations." Zuri agreed it was likely someone who was out to get Gigi, but they really did need to explore all the angles.

"Rachel Smith is our best lead. You should try to feel her out, Claudia," Julianna suggested.

Claudia groaned but nodded.

"One more thing, why do you have a baseball bat, Zuri? I thought you didn't play any sports." Julianna eyed the silver bat.

"I don't. It's a forget-me stick." Zuri pointed to the decal that read just that on the bat's side. "I was Megamind for an office Halloween party a few years ago. It's supposed to be black, but I didn't have time to paint it. Now I just keep it handy for situations like this."

"Do you have any photos?" Julianna shot up, her trademark grin spread across her face.

"Yeah, somewhere in the cloud, probably." She definitely had photos, but there was no way she was showing them. The costume had not come to life as well as she had hoped. It was embarrassing.

"We should definitely do a group Halloween costume." Julianna brought the tips of their fingers together like she was a cartoon villain plotting their next evil scheme.

She looked up at the clock. It was 3 a.m. They had only slept for a few hours. "Should we try to get some more sleep?" she suggested.

"I'll stay out here." Julianna yawned. "I'm too tired to move. But leave the forget-me stick."

She grabbed Julianna's drool-stained pillow and a blanket from the bedroom and threw them on top of her. Hopefully, they would find more answers in the morning.

Chapter 19

Monday

Thud.

The Grimoire sat on the counter in front of Violet, whose eyebrows shot to her hairline.

"How did you get this?" Violet's hands hovered over the thick cover.

"The less you know about that, the better." Claudia crossed her arms over her chest.

"And that's the dog?" Violet nodded at Gigi, who barked in return. This was only the third time Zuri had heard Gigi bark in the nearly two weeks since she'd gotten her. First at Dr. Smith, then at the robber, and now at Violet. As promised, she was otherwise a quiet and stoic dog.

"We searched for hours last night and this morning but found no spells about animals pooping gold."

Technically, she should be at work, but it had been a late night. She'd asked her boss to flex and work four tens that week. Claudia normally had Mondays off. Julianna. . . She still wasn't sure what Julianna did for a living, but as far as she could tell, Julianna hadn't needed to report to anyone that she wouldn't be in that day.

They'd brought Gigi with them, rather than risk her being stolen while she was alone. Gigi wouldn't get any closer and she emitted a low growl upon seeing Violet at the counter. Zuri had to pick her up just to get her into the shop, which was no easy feat, despite Gigi having lost weight.

"Well, what Astrid was doing was illegal, so of course she wouldn't put it out in the open."

Violet walked out from behind the counter and locked the shop door. She flipped the open sign to closed and shut the curtains before motioning for them to follow her to the back of the shop. She opened a door to what appeared to be a coat closet, but actually hid a staircase leading downward, similar to the one they had found at Astrid's place. The witch led the way down, with an excited Julianna at her heels and Claudia not far behind. Zuri hesitated, Gigi at her side.

She wasn't sure if it was a good idea to follow a witch into her magic basement that shouldn't even exist, especially after what they had seen in Astrid's basement. So far, the only other witch they knew about was an evil one. Violet might want to keep Gigi and the Grimoire and get rid of the only three people who would know she had them.

She hesitated, but it was their only chance to save Gigi. Or at least the only chance that they knew of. Hopefully, Violet wouldn't turn them into frogs or use them for some kind of ritual sacrifice. She started down the stairs, followed by a reluctant Gigi. The door slammed shut behind them.

Unlike Astrid's basement, Violet's didn't reek of decay and garbage. Instead, it smelled floral. The floors were clean. Instead of a crystal-like stone, the walls had cheerful wallpaper with violets printed on them. It was furnished with a comfortable looking, round, C-shaped black couch. An enormous cauldron sat in front of it, similar in size to Astrid's, along with a stand, holding what must be Violet's own Grimoire.

Julianna flopped down in the middle of the couch and Claudia, more gently, sat next to her. Gigi didn't want to move farther into the room, so she dropped the leash and sat down at one end. With the door to the stairs shut, Gigi couldn't go anywhere that Zuri wouldn't be able to see her and seemed more interested in avoiding Violet than a confrontation with the witch. In the end, she followed Zuri to the couch and sat at her feet.

Violet waved a finger, and her Grimoire lifted off the stand and into the drawer of a desk that sat along one wall. She placed Astrid's Grimoire on the stand before waving her hands over it and uttering

some words under her breath. The book opened
and pages turned in rapid succession before
the book closed again. Violet muttered under
her breath again, but this time, she only waved
two fingers. Again, the book opened, every page
fluttered, and the book slammed shut once more.

"Which one of you found the book?" Violet
turned to them.

"I did." Zuri raised a hand and immediately put
it back down. What was she, in grade school?

"How did it happen?"

She wasn't sure she could tell Violet without
also telling her about breaking into Astrid's house.
Claudia had been clear when they came in that
she didn't think Violet needed to know about their
tiny little misdemeanor adventure of breaking
and entering. At least she hoped it was only a
misdemeanor. Zuri wasn't really the lawbreaking
type, so she wasn't sure. She glanced over at
Claudia for permission to spill the details. Claudia
sighed before nodding.

"We found a magic basement like this in Astrid's
house, although yours is much nicer," she started.

"So much nicer," Claudia mumbled under her
breath.

"Anyway, the book floated toward me when I
reached for it. I grabbed it and we left."

"How did you get out of the basement?" Violet looked skeptical.

"We don't know. The door disappeared and then it reappeared. Magic." She made jazz hands in emphasis.

"Think harder. You had to have done something. A witch wouldn't leave her workshop without wards to keep intruders out. Only another witch should've been able to find the workshop in the first place, and it would definitely take one to get out." Violet stared at her.

It had only been the three of them, and only Claudia and Zuri had been in the basement.

"Zuri, you're the one who found the door to the basement," Julianna stated. "I didn't even see that door until you opened it."

"You're also the one who opened the book last night," Claudia reminded her.

"How did you get out of the basement?" Violet repeated.

Zuri shook her head again. "I don't know. I was scared. I closed my eyes and just wished really hard that the door would come back and open. "

Violet stared at her with wide eyes. The room was quiet. Zuri looked down at Gigi, but Gigi only looked back with a bored expression. She was no help.

"You're a sprout." Violet continued to stare at her. "Or you've got magic in your family."

"What's a sprout?" Claudia asked.

"New magic." A smile lit up Violet's face. It was the first time they had seen her looking this happy since they had mentioned Astrid's death. It was scary.

"New magic?" She looked down at Gigi.

"You're a wizard, Zuri!" Julianna yelled.

"Being around that enchanted dog might have activated your magic, though we'll probably never know exactly what triggered it." Violet looked confident, like she just knew Zuri was a witch. No questions. Zuri wasn't so sure. It was one thing to have an enchanted dog, it was another thing to suddenly have magic powers.

"Look, can you explain this to us from the beginning, please? Other than what you already told us about the coins, we don't know anything about witches or magic," Claudia asked.

Violet took a seat on the couch, but it was obvious she was still having a hard time sitting still. She was excited. Hopefully, for a reason that was good for them and Gigi.

"It's not that complicated. You've seen plenty of movies and books with magical worlds. Some hidden, and others blended with the regular human world. Where do you think the ideas came from?" Violet started.

"Our existences have always been intertwined with non-magical humans. To prevent both regular humans and overzealous witches from using our power for their own personal gain, we've long lived parallel but separate. We have our own societies and governments who make laws and rules to keep everyone safe."

Violet waved her finger in circles, and steaming teacups and saucers appeared in the air in front of them. Trays of scones and shortbread cookies levitated within reach. This wasn't like when she made books move or pages flip open without touching them. She made the food appear out of thin air.

"Sorry, all this talking is making me thirsty. Time for tea." She took a sip from the delicate-looking teacup. The set was white with a floral pattern, more violets.

"Can I get some milk? And sugar." Julianna grinned at her tea. Violet waved a finger, obliging.

"Magic runs in families, but every once in a while, it will choose to plant a seed of itself in someone new. That's why we call it a sprout. Like a seed, the magic doesn't always germinate. In your case, if indeed there is no one in your family who could have passed on magic to you, then you are a sprout." Violet took another sip of tea.

"Would I know if someone in my family had magic? What if they just never told me?" Zuri stared at the floor, still not fully convinced of her magical abilities. It wasn't like she was an orphan. She wasn't close to her parents, at least not now, but she was pretty sure neither of them had an ounce of magic in them.

Her mom. . . Well, if her mom had magic, she would know. Her mother had lived a hard life, partially of her own making. If she had magic, she would have used it to make her life easier without a spare thought.

She didn't know her father well. Her parents had separated before she even finished elementary school. Still, he'd been around long enough that she was sure she would remember if he'd ever used magic around the house. She remembered him being kind and him playing games with her outside, but definitely no magic.

Maybe having spent so much time with Gigi, Astrid's wards and her Grimoire had gotten confused. Maybe some of Astrid's power had simply been clinging to her. That seemed more logical than Zuri being a witch herself.

"Of course they would tell you. Magic runs in families. It's the family's responsibility to teach their children the basics."

"Is it possible that it skipped a generation or two?" Zuri asked.

"Unlikely." Violet finished her tea and pushed her cup and saucer away before standing and walking back to Astrid's Grimoire. "Come here and open the book."

"What? Why can't you just do it?" Zuri asked. A wave of heat washed over her and her heart started pounding in her chest.

"If I could, I would have. You already unlocked Astrid's wards once without knowing what you were doing. If you try, I'm sure you can unlock the ones hiding her illegal spells."

"I don't think—"

"Get over here and try," Violet commanded, interrupting her.

She glanced over at the other women. Julianna was too invested in devouring an entire tray of cookies to offer any help. Claudia motioned for her to get up. She looked at Gigi, but the dog had laid down and closed her eyes. No one was going to save her. Typical. Reluctantly, she moved to stand next to Violet in front of the Grimoire.

"You said you wished really hard for the basement door to reappear, and it did. Try that with the Grimoire. Think really hard about unlocking the wards." Violet motioned toward the book with an open palm.

"Shouldn't we start with something easier? Assuming I even have any magic?" This didn't seem like a good idea. Magic powers sounded fun in theory, but Zuri could think of 100 ways this could go wrong. She rubbed her now sweaty palms against her jeans.

"Give it a shot," Violet urged. "While I'm here to help contain things, the worst thing that can happen is that nothing will happen."

Zuri turned toward the Grimoire and closed her eyes. *Crunch.* She tried to focus on the book and whether the wards would look like locks. *Crunch.* She took a breath and tried to visualize the wards again. *Crunch.*

"Do you mind?" she shouted at Julianna, who held a cookie a few inches from her mouth while her other hand reached for a second one.

"Sorry." Julianna sheepishly put both cookies down and brushed the crumbs off her fingers, sitting at attention.

Again, she closed her eyes and focused, imagining the locks. *Open. Show us the spell that enchanted Gigi.* She silently repeated this will to herself for what felt like forever.

Crunch.

Her eyes flew open. She turned to glare at Julianna.

"What? You're done, so I can eat again." She pointed to the book with her cookie before squealing with delight, stomping her feet on the floor.

Zuri looked in front of her. The book was open. The page title read, *Golden Life: Turn Life Force into Gold.*

She did it. She unlocked the wards. Magic was real. To be fair, that was already established. But Zuri had magic. She had magic. *Magic.*

Turning, she looked at Claudia, who looked back at her, eyes wide and eyebrows creeping toward her hairline. She faced Violet, who gave her a knowing glance before stepping up to read the spell.

"So why didn't she have to say any magic words or wave her finger like you?" Claudia asked, an eye for detail. Now Zuri wondered too. Nothing she had done felt special. How could it have been that easy?

Violet looked up from the book.

"There are three types of witches." She held up one finger. "Those who need an object to help them focus their magic. They can't use magic without the object, and such objects are not cheap or easy to come by." A second finger. "Then, there are witches like me, who use words or movement to focus our magic. Most powerful are witches like. . . I'm sorry, what were your names again?" Violet looked confused. It was clear that she had not believed they were coming back and so had not even attempted to remember their names from the last time they'd met.

"Zuri. I'm Zuri. That's Claudia, and that's Julianna." She pointed at herself and her friends.

"Zuri." Violet nodded.

"Are you saying Zuri is not only a witch, but a powerful one?" Julianna asked, her eyes sparkling with joy.

"Yes. With some training, I suspect she'll be a *very powerful* one." Violet frowned and looked into the distance. "But right now, untrained and knowing so little, you're a danger to yourself and others. I'll need to tell the Witch's Council about you. It's been a long time since we had a sprout in this territory." Violet returned her attention to the book. "But first, let's disenchant your dog."

"Can't we just undo the spell like we did the wards?" Claudia questioned.

"Magic cast on objects is a little different from magic cast on living things. We could try, but in this case, the magic is linked to Gigi's life force. If we make a mistake, it might cost her life." Violet ran a finger beneath the text on the spell's page.

Zuri read over her shoulder.

Golden Life: Turn Life Force into Gold
Ingredients
1 Cauldron Basic Brew Stock
1 Witch's Coin
5 Money Tree Leaves

4 drops of water from a wish fountain
3 hot river rocks
2 bottled millionaire sighs
1 living sacrifice

Brew all ingredients except the living sacrifice, continuing to stir until bubbling. At the stroke of midnight, repeat the incantation: This life has no value but value it will create. I trade it for gold, two coins for one pound of weight.

Bottle the potion. One serving size is eight ounces. You can store unused portions for up to four full moons.

Make sure the living sacrifice drinks the entire serving of the potion.

Notes: Results may vary.

Wait. Two coins for every pound of weight? Gigi was fifty-four pounds when she had her first vet visit and Zuri had twenty coins. Ten pounds. She pooped four gold coins at a time. If they didn't reverse this soon. . .

Zuri looked at Gigi.

"What's wrong?" Claudia asked.

Zuri didn't answer. She just shook her head before turning around to pace. This couldn't be right. Her mind flashed back to the pile of animal bones in Astrid's basement.

Claudia and Julianna got up and went to the Grimoire, but not without trying to push each other out of the way. The room was silent for a few minutes.

"We don't have a lot of time." Julianna broke the quiet.

Chapter 20

Stars and a bright moon lit up the clear sky by the time they left Violet's workshop.

Violet was a cautious witch. She wanted to find the exact replacement ingredients that would counter the ones used in the potion, but it required a lot of research. They spent hours comparing the original potion ingredients to the old books in Violet's personal library. The problem was that the answer changed depending on which book you asked. Every witch seemed to have had their own experiences and ideas on what ingredients counteracted others.

Fortunately, she had something else in mind. Every month on the night of the full moon, Violet and a few other witches snuck into a community pool to go skinny-dipping. According to her, it had nothing to do with magic or being a witch. It was just fun. Apparently, it was even more fun getting caught and pretending that, because of their age, they didn't know how they had gotten there. Violet laughed and laughed as she remembered the police officers' faces.

This time, she would discretely get some advice from her witch friends. Zuri had asked to join her, but Violet refused. First because she didn't think anyone should know about Zuri until after she had a chance to meet with the Witch's Council. Second, because it had been her choice to reveal herself to the three of them as a witch, but she couldn't out others. There could be consequences. Violet didn't elaborate on what those consequences might be, but Zuri honestly didn't want to find out.

They made the quick trip back to Zuri's place. While Julianna went through Zuri's kitchen to make them dinner, Zuri and Claudia took Gigi for a quick loop around the neighborhood. When they got back, the house was alive with the scent of garlic. Julianna had even set the table with three plates, forks, and glasses of water.

"Mmm, that smells so good. What are you making?" Zuri yelled from the doorway while unclasping Gigi's leash.

"Just spaghetti and garlic bread. We need all the carbs to fight evil," Julianna replied.

Zuri and Claudia sat at the kitchen island. Zuri watched Gigi sink onto the cool tile floor next to the kitchen sink. As long as Claudia and Julianna ignored her, Gigi didn't seem to mind that they were there.

"So. . ." Julianna started as she drained the pasta in the sink. "You want to try doing some more magic?" She turned and grinned at Zuri expectantly.

"You heard Violet. I'm currently a danger to myself and others. I don't think it's a good idea." Zuri slumped in her chair.

She glanced at Claudia, expecting some backup. Instead, Claudia bit her lip, a small smile forming at the corner of her mouth.

"Seriously, Claudia? I expected this from Julianna, but you?" Zuri crossed her arms over her chest.

"What if we just try something small?" Claudia turned toward her. "Like levitating this spoon." She pushed the spoon to the center of the table.

Zuri looked at the spoon and sighed. On the one hand, this was still a bad idea. On the other hand, what if Violet was wrong and Zuri wasn't a witch at all? What if she underestimated how much of Astrid's magic might have just rubbed off onto her from Gigi? If she were a teenager, she might have believed she had magic, but she couldn't think of a single example of a character in one of her books or movies getting magic in their thirties. She had to know.

Just like she had in the basement of Violet's workshop, she closed her eyes and focused. She imagined the spoon levitating off the table. Not hearing anything, she opened her eyes. The spoon sat exactly where it had in front of her.

"See, nothing. Violet was wrong." Zuri shrugged before slouching back into her chair. She didn't have magic. She wasn't special.

"Try again," Claudia said softly. She looked up and Julianna nodded.

Groaning, Zuri closed her eyes again and sat up straight. Thinking back to some of the breathing exercises she learned in therapy, she tried to slow her breath and thoughts down. It took a moment, but she blocked everything else out and imagined the spoon levitating again. Just her and the spoon. *Rise*, she commanded it.

Bang!

Her eyes flew open, but the spoon was gone. She looked around and caught a glimpse of Gigi scrambling from the kitchen to her bed in the living room.

"Where—" she started, but her eyes followed Claudia's gaze to the ceiling, where the spoon was now lodged like a dart in a target board.

Zuri couldn't deny it now. She had magic. What was she supposed to do with it? Usually, when this happened in books or movies, the main character was some kind of chosen one, destined to fight a big, evil boss. All she wanted to do was disenchant her Chow so she could return to her quiet life of reading on the couch and drinking tea. No magic was required for that dream. Although she guessed if she could summon tea and cookies out of thin air like Violet, that would be pretty cool. Maybe some treats for Gigi too, if she would eat them, though her daily steak had likely spoiled her by now.

"Are we just going to leave it up there?" Claudia asked.

"Should I try to get it down?" she asked no one in particular, but Claudia and Julianna both shook their heads.

"No, you were right. This is too dangerous." Claudia turned toward her empty plate.

"But—" Julianna started to protest, but Claudia cut her off.

"Imagine if that had hit one of us."

That made Julianna close her mouth, but Zuri thought it was more because she knew she wouldn't win, rather than because she was worried about being hit by flying projectiles. Julianna plated their meal, and they dug in.

"So, what are we doing about potential middle of the night dog knappers? Are we sleeping over again?" Julianna asked.

"You and Gigi shouldn't stay here until we disenchant her," Claudia started. "You should stay with me or Julianna. It'll make it harder for whoever is after Gigi to find her."

"I know your place is smaller, Claudia, but Gigi and my cats definitely won't get along," Julianna stated.

"Yeah, I thought that might be the case. It's fine. They can stay with me." She took another bite of garlic bread.

"You don't. . . I mean, you've both already done so much. . . I don't want to impose." Zuri started looking down at her plate.

"You're not," Claudia stated.

Zuri could feel both their eyes on her. She liked Claudia. A lot. More than she should. She liked Julianna too. They were both fun to be around. She was also a little jealous at how they seemed to move through every situation with ease. Of course they were right that it was too dangerous to stay at her condo with someone after Gigi, but it would be so awkward and uncomfortable to stay at someone else's house, especially Claudia's. Her social battery was already at zero after the last twenty-four hours.

"I could always go to a hotel," Zuri suggested. She chanced a look up. Claudia's lips formed a tight line of disapproval while Julianna looked amused.

"You don't know if they have a way to track you and Gigi. Do you really want to be alone if they find you?" Claudia stared at her.

"No, but this isn't your problem. You don't have to keep helping me." Zuri stirred the spaghetti around on her plate. It wasn't just the thought of staying at someone else's house that was bothering her. It just felt weird, being on the receiving end of help. Especially since she didn't know them that well. Normally, she was the one doing the helping. It started with her mom, but even with other friends, back when she'd had friends, and with relationships. She always helped, but when she was struggling, she never asked, and no one offered. The squeaky wheels got the grease, and she wasn't a squeaky wheel.

"We *want* to help you." Claudia rolled her eyes.

"Yeah." Julianna smiled, no hint of mischief this time.

"It's settled. Julianna and I will clean up after dinner, and you can pack some clothes and your work laptop. I'd offer to drive you home Jules, but I know you're going to call your own ride." Claudia picked up her fork again, signaling the end of the discussion.

Zuri wasn't sure how to feel. Part of her was relieved that she wouldn't have to navigate the new world of magic and witches alone. But she was also still nervous about being alone with Claudia, and at Claudia's house. At least at her house, Zuri was in the one place where she could relax. At someone else's house, though. . . She was going to be so uncomfortable.

Gigi sighed and Zuri turned to meet her eyes. They agreed. Neither one of them was going to like this.

An hour later, Julianna went home and Claudia drove them to her "apartment." It was really a 450 square foot guesthouse in her parents' backyard. As they pulled into the driveway, Zuri glanced anxiously at the larger house.

"Don't worry, no one's home." Claudia turned off the engine.

"Where is everyone?" Zuri asked, hoping she wouldn't have to meet Claudia's family anytime soon. It wasn't that she was afraid of meeting them, it was just that she was worried about feeling awkward. Well, more awkward. The time spent at Violet's and the night before with Julianna and Claudia was still swimming in her head. So much to process already. There just wasn't room for any new interactions.

"My parents are on a cruise right now and my sister is at a conference this week. She's traveling for work next week, directly from the conference." She led the way through the gate and to the small white guesthouse. Zuri and Gigi followed, but Zuri had to stop every few feet for Gigi to smell something.

It was actually bigger on the inside than it looked. A small red love seat facing a thirty-two-inch TV mounted on the wall made up the living room. A small desk and chair encompassed a home office by the wall behind the couch. The kitchen was small, but a generous island that doubled as a table with four chairs added to the counter space.

"It's tiny, but the couch is a pullout." Claudia put her work bag down next to the door and took her shoes off.

"It's really nice. Thanks again for letting us stay." Zuri put Gigi's dog bed and her backpack on the floor before taking her shoes off. She hadn't brought much. Two pairs of clothes and one set of pajamas. She'd brought Gigi's water bowl and one of her dog beds. Hopefully, they wouldn't be staying too long. As soon as Gigi was disenchanted, no one would have any reason to steal her. They could go home.

"Oh, I almost forgot." Claudia stooped down and rummaged through her work bag. She stood, pulling out a familiar-looking bag of tea. "I stole this from your kitchen. I really liked it when you made it last night. I figured it might help you feel more comfortable." She smiled, taking the bag to the kitchen.

"Thank you," Zuri replied, a little stunned. She hadn't even thought to bring any. That was so thoughtful, and it would make her feel better.

"I'm going to take a shower, but make yourself at home." Claudia made a beeline for a door down a small hallway that must have been the bathroom.

Zuri went to the kitchen and filled Gigi's bowl with water, placing it next to the island and hopefully out of the way. She moved Gigi's dog bed next to the desk along the wall. Gigi took that as an invitation and laid in it immediately.

Bending down, Zuri pet Gigi's neck and watched her stretch her arms out as if she were Superman, flying in the sky.

"You're going to be able to eat and poop like a normal dog again soon, just wait and see," Zuri whispered. Gigi's ears flicked up at the sound of her voice, but Zuri could tell she was only listening for the magic word, "steak." Unless it was about steak or going to the park, Gigi didn't really seem to care what Zuri was saying.

Satisfied that Gigi was comfortable, or at least as comfortable as she could be at that moment, Zuri changed into her pajamas. She looked around, but Claudia's apartment was, unsurprisingly, very neat and tidy. She didn't have any clutter or knickknacks. The only photos on the wall were of Claudia and a gray cat and a couple of family photos of Claudia, her parents, and her two siblings. The cat must have been Charlotte. Most of the few photos hanging around were of her.

Zuri had only known Gigi a couple weeks, but she knew it would leave a giant hole in her heart if she didn't figure out how to save her. She couldn't imagine what Claudia must feel after having lost Charlotte, whom she'd had for so much longer.

Turning away from the photos, she sat on the couch and closed her eyes. The last twenty-four or so hours had been unreal. Her brain felt like it was overheating as dozens of images replayed in her head. It was too much.

A distraction. That's what she needed. She grabbed the remote off the round coffee table in front of her and switched on the TV. She clicked on the app for Disney+ but Claudia wasn't logged in, so she had to put in her own username and password. In the "continue watching" section, she quickly found what she was looking for and flicked the next episode on.

Zuri had already seen this episode, but not in a while. She was so wrapped up in the show; she didn't hear when Claudia exited the bathroom and returned to the living room.

"*What* are you watching?" Claudia stated in mock disgust, but she heard the smile in her voice.

"It's *The Owl House*. It's great. I can start it over for you, if you want." Zuri turned to look at Claudia.

Her dark shoulder-length hair was still wet. Her pajamas consisted of an oversized black T-shirt and pink plaid pants. The light from the TV screen reflected in her glasses. Those were new.

"It's a cartoon." Claudia walked around to sit on the couch next to Zuri.

"It's amazing. You're going to love it." Zuri paused the show.

"What's it about?"

"Found family. Finding your place in the world. Coming of age. Friendship! It has all the good stuff." Zuri grinned.

Claudia let out a mock sigh. "Fine, but only because I don't think I've ever seen you this excited about something before, and it's kind of cute."

She restarted the series from episode one while trying to calm the thundering boom of her heart thumping in her chest. Hopefully, it was only her who could hear it. She dared a quick glance at Claudia and noted a slight pink on her cheeks. Zuri would never know for sure, but maybe that last part she hadn't meant to say out loud.

They watched the rest of the episode in a comfortable silence.

Chapter 21

Nothing. Two days and they'd figured out nothing. Gigi hadn't pooped any more coins, but Zuri also hadn't had the heart to feed her. Gigi was lethargic, mostly just sleeping all day. She stayed close to Zuri, keeping her within sight. She even followed Zuri into the bathroom, which said a lot about Gigi's mental state.

On both days, Claudia woke up early to go running before going to the clinic. Both times, Zuri woke up with her. She was quiet, but Zuri was still on high alert after the break-in. She waited until the front door clicked shut and then shuffled out of bed herself.

While Claudia worked at the clinic, Zuri worked at Claudia's desk. It wasn't ideal, not having a second monitor, but it also wasn't that big of a deal. She didn't want to risk going back to her place, even if her car was still there.

Julianna came over the previous afternoon and made dinner for the three of them. It was ready on the island table when Claudia walked in after work. Then they waited, hoping that Violet would call with some news. She hadn't yet. Their efforts to find anything useful online hadn't yielded any fruit either.

Zuri sat with her back against the living room wall, absently stroking Gigi's soft fur. Gigi's eyes were closed, but Zuri knew she was awake because she wasn't snoring. The rumbling snores that had once startled her were now comforting background noise the she'd grown fond of. Every once in a while, Gigi would stretch her arms forward, flexing her cute, little black paws.

The black bear of a dog had hardly moved during the day while Zuri had been working. She took a few steps away from the guesthouse at five o'clock to do her business, drank some water, and went back to bed. Zuri couldn't wait until Gigi was cured of the enchantment. She would buy her all the best dog treats, chicken, steak, whatever Gigi wanted.

It was almost time for Claudia to get back. Julianna pranced around the kitchen and Zuri smelled something delicious for dinner again. Julianna was a surprisingly good cook. On both days, she walked in with grocery bags and made herself at home in Claudia's kitchen.

Leaving Gigi to relax, Zuri stood and wandered over to the island. Eggplant Parmesan sizzled in a skillet on the stove. An empty bag of cheese laid on the counter and there were breadcrumbs everywhere.

While Julianna could cook, she did not clean up after herself very well. The night before, Zuri and Claudia had tag teamed the kitchen after Julianna went home. It looked like they would be doing that again. Not that Zuri minded.

"That smells amazing." Zuri nearly drooled.

"I know." Julianna smiled. Not a humble bone in her body.

Claudia opened the front door just as Julianna was taking the food out of the oven.

"Perfect timing." Julianna began plating the food.

"Perfect indeed. I'm starving." Claudia dropped her work bag by the door and took a seat next to Zuri at the table. Julianna slid their plates across the island and walked around it to join them.

Zuri spared a guilty glance toward Gigi, before she started shoveling her food into her mouth.

"Any news?" Claudia turned to look at Zuri.

She shook her head. Zuri had called Violet at lunch, after Old Gold had opened, but the witch was still trying to figure out the counter potion and spell.

"What about you? Did you find anything out about Rachel?" She tried not to get her hopes up.

Claudia shook her head.

"She called out sick again today."

"We should pay her a visit. You know, pretend to bring her soup or something." Julianna winked.

"I might have broken into HR's computer while they were at lunch. They never remember to lock it.. She gave a fake address. It's a grocery store when you google it." Claudia grimaced.

"We've been spending too much time together. I think I'm rubbing off on you." Julianna smiled.

Her heart sank at the news. It would at least be nice to know for sure who was trying to steal Gigi. If they knew for sure who it was, maybe they could do something about it. They could report them to the Witch's Council. Or something. There had to be something. But without knowing...

Claudia nudged Zuri's shoulder.

"Want to watch *The Owl House* after dinner?"

She was trying to cheer her up. She wouldn't even admit she liked it yet, but Zuri knew she did. Claudia was always the one to hit the next episode, and she never suggested switching to a different show or movie.

"What's *The Owl House*?" Julianna walked around the counter to grab seconds.

"It's a cartoon about a human girl who wants to be a witch, and she stumbles into a magical world." Claudia slid her plate across to Julianna for seconds.

Julianna looked between them before putting another piece of breaded eggplant and sauce on her and Claudia's plates.

"What?" Zuri smiled. "It's a good show!"

Julianna snorted, amused.

The rest of the night went similarly to the day before. After dinner, Julianna went home to spend time with her cats and do whatever it was she didn't want Zuri to know about. Claudia and Zuri cleaned the kitchen and watched a few episodes of *The Owl House*. They took turns showering. They walked Gigi in Claudia's yard together.

As much as she enjoyed living alone, if she had to live with someone, she really liked living with Claudia. Unlike her previous roommates, Claudia was clean and organized. Although they weren't on the same schedule, Claudia, an early bird ready to seize the day, and Zuri, a night owl, somehow they still just worked. Over the last couple of days, they seamlessly settled into a routine together. Rather than the usual awkwardness of being in someone else's space, Zuri quickly felt at ease in Claudia's home. Relaxed.

"Did you get to live back here when you were growing up?" Zuri locked the front door.

"No. My parents built this for me after I got into vet school. They bribed me to come back with free rent." Claudia removed the red couch cushions and pulled the bed out for Zuri. "They travel a lot, so they wanted to make sure someone would be home to watch the house."

So, she was close to her family. Well of course she was. She lived in their backyard. That was nice.

"What about you? Does your family live close?"

"No," Zuri answered without further explanation or details. She quickly walked the short distance to the bedroom and grabbed a pillow. She dragged her feet a little on the trip back to the living room, but there was no need. Claudia was good like that. She respected boundaries. Zuri really liked that about her. It was a rare trait to find, honestly.

It didn't take Zuri long to fall asleep, despite Gigi's snoring. Zuri didn't dream often, but when she did, they were vivid and sometimes terrifying dreams where she woke shaking and sweating. Unfortunately, that night, she was met with such dreams. She didn't know where she was. It was dark and cold. She saw and felt an electric shock go through her. She couldn't move. She was paralyzed. An old woman screamed at her but she couldn't make out a word. A young blonde woman laughed at her. A red ruby ring. She opened her eyes, but she was still stuck in place, unable to move.

Breathe. She kept trying to inhale, but she couldn't make her lungs take a breath. Was this it? Was this how it ended? Panic made her heart race, but no matter how hard she tried, she couldn't move. She laid there, immobile for what felt like forever, until suddenly she could breathe again. It took her a few minutes to get the rest of her body with the program. She moved her fingers first and then her toes. Finally, she could move her arms.

Zuri sat up. The front door was wide open. She looked down. Gigi wasn't in her bed, where she had been when Zuri had gone to sleep. She stepped out of bed and looked around the room. No Gigi.

She ran out the door but saw nothing or anyone. The night air felt still. Not even the crickets were chirping.

Running back inside, Zuri checked every corner of the house before she ran to Claudia's room.

"Claudia!" Claudia didn't move. Zuri shook her, tears now streaming down her face.

"Claudia!"

Claudia gasped, taking a big inhale and shooting up to a sitting position.

"Claudia, she's gone." Zuri collapsed onto the floor next to the bed. Claudia crawled out from under the blankets and knelt beside her, putting her hands on Zuri's shoulders.

"What do you mean? What happened?"

"Gigi is gone. They took her." She lost all control, all the stress from the last week finally catching up with her. She sobbed uncontrollably as Claudia held her.

After everything, Gigi was gone.

Chapter 22

Friday

It was two a.m. when Zuri woke up from her sleep paralysis nightmare to find Gigi gone. Neither she nor Claudia had gone back to sleep. Claudia let her cry for a little while and then she made her get up, wash her face, and get dressed. Claudia called Julianna and even Violet to fill them in on what happened.

Claudia wanted to call the police, but Violet said witches had their own people to investigate magical crimes. The regular police would be of no use. Not that Zuri would have been crazy about calling them anyway. There were worse police departments, but that didn't mean she necessarily felt safe calling hers as a brown person. The consequences of calling versus not calling always had to be weighed. She hoped that somehow, the magical investigators from the Witch's Council would be better. Since she didn't know much about witch politics or society, though, it was just a risk they going to have to take.

An hour after getting off the phone, Violet arrived at Claudia's house with two unfamiliar faces. A short, middle-aged man with a dark complexion and a very tall, older, tanned woman with long silver hair. They wore matching black suite, even down to their shoes. They reminded Zuri of the *Men in Black*. Hopefully, they didn't intend to use the flashy thing on her.

"Remarkable," the woman murmured, stepping into Zuri's bubble. She leaned down, bringing her face inches from Zuri's and staring straight into her eyes. Zuri felt frozen, unable to look away, despite the uncomfortable closeness of the stranger.

Violet coughed, a small attempt to rein the strange woman in, but it went ignored.

"Lucy, you're scaring the poor girl." Violet clucked, shooing the woman away from Zuri.

"She's just boiling with magic. Coming off her like steam." The woman, apparently Lucy, continued to study Zuri, stepping closer again.

"Are these the special investigators you mentioned over the phone?" Claudia motioned for the three witches to sit down at the bar counter. The man nodded to her and sat down. Violet had to physically grab Lucy's arm to get her to move away from Zuri.

"These are investigators Lucy Alba and Michael Green, from the Witch's Council's Department of

Special Investigations for crimes against other witches," Violet introduced her companions.

Claudia put on her kettle and started her coffee maker. They weren't going back to sleep, so they might as well start caffeinating. She supposed they could have asked Violet to use her magic to make coffee or tea appear, but Claudia was probably trying to be a good host by making it herself.

Zuri hovered in the kitchen near the counter, glad there was something between her and Lucy's intense gaze.

"Violet tells us you adopted a dog that made gold, and it was stolen a couple hours ago?" Michael pulled out a notebook, looking at Zuri.

She told them everything from the beginning. How she'd gotten Gigi from the shelter. The gold coins. Getting the Grimoire. The fake animal control officer. The failed burglary. The sleep paralysis and her dream. She left nothing out. She didn't care if they got in trouble with the regular human police or the Witch's Council at this point. All that mattered was finding Gigi and breaking the spell.

The investigators kept their faces impassive the entire time. Michael never took out a pen, but Zuri noticed the notebook page was filled word for word and line by line with her words, verbatim. Practical magic. That would have been useful when she was back in college. Even the AI generated transcripts available now weren't that accurate.

"Violet." Michael looked over at the woman, a bored expression painted on his face.

"I was going to file a report." Her face was the picture of innocence. "I just wanted to help them disenchant the dog first. The poor thing is days away from expiring."

"So, you weren't planning to keep Astrid's Grimoire?" A smug smile crept into the corners of his mouth.

"Why, I would never." Violet shook her head and brought a hand to her chest in indignation.

Michael clearly didn't believe her, but he didn't press the matter.

"First things first." Lucy finally stopped staring at Zuri, or rather the magic that was apparently emanating from Zuri. "We need to locate the dog and whoever took her."

"Right. They'll probably be looking to replicate that illegal spell of Astrid's." Michael stood.

He rubbed a gold ring. A gold ring with a red ruby. The ring.

"The ring, in my dream, it looked like yours." Zuri eyed it suspiciously.

"This is a power stone. Neither the type of stone nor the design are unique. You'll start to notice others around you wearing them." Michael didn't look offended at her question.

"I thought you said those types of objects weren't easy to come by." Claudia looked at Violet, who was sipping her coffee now.

"The stones are difficult to find and mine, so they're rather pricey, but those in the same affinity tend to choose similar designs."

A short, urgent sounding chime rang out.

"Gah!" Violet shrieked. "Someone's trying to get past my wards at my sanctuary."

"You mean your secret magic basement?" Claudia began walking toward the door.

"It's not a *basement*, it's a sanctuary, and YES." The three witches rose, moving toward the door.

"We'll meet you there." Zuri and Claudia got halfway down the driveway to Claudia's car before Zuri felt a sharp yank at the collar of her shirt. It was Lucy.

"You two will wait here. We'll update you when we have more information about your dog."

"But—"

"No buts." Michael stopped next to Lucy. "It could be dangerous."

"You don't want to disobey an order from a Witch's Council Investigator. Trust me." Violet made a face like she had some experience in this department.

They watched as the trio got into a black sedan and speedily drove away.

"We're still going to the shop, right?" she asked.

Instead of the answer she wanted, she felt Claudia's arms wrap around her.

"No, we're going to wait."

She tried to pull out of Claudia's grasp so she could face her, but Claudia doubled down, tightening her hold.

"I know you're worried about Gigi, but I don't want you to get in trouble with the Witch's Council. Especially when we don't even know much about them."

"But—" Zuri started, before she was interrupted a second time.

"Think about it. What if they put you in witch jail or something? Or worse. What if it is too dangerous and you end up hurt? Who would take care of Gigi then?"

Zuri took in a deep breath. She let her body relax as she exhaled.

"These are dangerous people. We don't even know what they're capable of. We know that they're willing to kill to get this witch's gold. You saw the pile of bones in Astrid's basement. If they want this spell so bad, they're likely ready to create a pile of their own."

She knew Claudia was right, but that didn't mean she liked it. This time, when she tried to pull out of Claudia's arms, she let her.

Zuri turned back toward the house, slowing so her friend could catch up and walk beside her.

Claudia cleared her throat. "Sorry for just grabbing you."

Zuri glanced at her through the corner of her eyes. As they neared the glow of the light next to the door, she could see Claudia's cheeks had turned a bright pink.

Under other circumstances, she would have felt her heart flutter in response. Now though, she just wanted to wake up from this nightmare.

Claudia steered Zuri toward the sofa. After calling Violet for backup, she had put the bed away and remade the couch. She grabbed Zuri's phone off the side table and handed it to her.

"You should probably let your boss know you won't be working today." She walked around the love seat and sat down at the other end. "I'm going to do the same."

"But if Rachel is involved, will they have someone who can cover for both of you?" Zuri surprised herself by asking. Some part of her brain was still capable of functioning.

Scrunching up her face, Claudia stopped typing. Zuri knew she was right.

"You should get some sleep," Zuri whispered. Their eyes met, and Zuri held Claudia's gaze.

Claudia knew what was happening, even before Zuri had completely realized it herself. Zuri felt the hair raise on her arms. She knew what she was doing, even if she didn't understand how she was doing it. If she wanted to, she might be able to stop it. If she wanted to, but she didn't.

Within seconds, Claudia's body went limp. Her breath rose and fell softly. Her head tilted back over the edge of the love seat.

Rising off the couch, Zuri closed her eyes and imagined Claudia safely tucked into her bed. She opened her eyes and peeked into the bedroom, seeing it was so. Sort of. Claudia's feet were on her pillow instead of her head. She was facing the wrong way. Carefully, Zuri grabbed the pillow and placed it under Claudia's head. She got Claudia's phone and put it on the bed next to her. Hopefully, her alarm would wake her up. It wasn't like Zuri's intention was for Claudia to sleep forever, just long enough that Zuri could go to the shop and find Gigi. If the alarm failed to wake her up, Violet and the investigators would have to help. They wouldn't just leave her like that. She hoped.

Walking back to the front door, Zuri grabbed Claudia's car keys off the hook. Dangerous or not, she was going to get her dog.

This was not what she had been expecting. Not even close. Instead of finding Rachel and the fake officer at Violet's shop, Zuri watched from the window of Claudia's car as another witch in a black suit led them out of the shop. Astrid. Zuri recognized her from the photos in her house. Astrid, who was supposed to be dead. Astrid, the reason Gigi was taken to the shelter in the first place.

Gigi!

Zuri leapt from the car and pushed past investigator Michael and then Lucy, flying down the stairs of Violet's sanctuary. Before she got to the bottom, Violet stopped her. Not physically. Although Zuri was short, Violet was petite. There was no way she could hold Zuri under normal circumstances. She blocked Zuri with some kind of invisible magic force field.

Zuri pushed against it with her own magic. She felt it surge under her skin and it crackled beneath her fingertips. It had never felt like this before. Or maybe she just hadn't allowed herself to feel it when she still didn't want to believe it was there. Now she did. Closing her eyes, she let the magic takeover. It knew what it was doing. She felt the break in Violet's barrier.

Violet shrieked as the force of Zuri's blow shoved her backward against the wall.

Zuri finished the climb down the stairs and stopped in her tracks. There, in front of the couch, was the perfectly laid out skeleton of a medium-sized dog. Like the pile of bones in Astrid's basement, it sat motionless and lifeless. No flesh clung to it and there was no blood or any other sign that the creature had been alive recently.

"I'm sorry, Zuri." Violet stood back up, walking closer.

"Is that. . ." She couldn't finish her sentence. She stared at the bones.

"We believe so." Violet gently grabbed Zuri's elbow. Another hand grabbed her other elbow. Investigator Michael. She allowed herself to be led up the stairs.

"We believe after stealing your dog, Astrid came here to get her Grimoire," Michael stated.

"But why. . ." Again, Zuri couldn't bring herself to say all the words out loud.

"When she realized she was caught, she tried to get rid of any evidence," Michael continued.

"But she was dead. Astrid was dead." Zuri kept her gaze on the floor. It just didn't make sense.

"She was never dead. She faked her death to begin a new life under a new identity to avoid paying human or witch taxes. The Witch's Council was getting suspicious about her increasing wealth. She was trying to avoid an investigation."

Zuri stood there, gaze on the floor. This could not be possible. That wasn't Gigi on the sanctuary floor. It wasn't. It couldn't be. Zuri's breath became ragged and short. A flame of power ignited in her heart, filling her chest with heat. Electricity zapped underneath her fingertips as she clenched her fists.

Astrid was going to pay for this. Zuri started toward the doors. If Astrid wasn't still out there, Zuri would find her, one way or another. It was time to see how *she* liked pooping gold coins until she died from starvation. *This life has no value, but value it will create.* Astrid's life was the only one without value. If all she could think to do with all the magic and power at her fingertips was to get rich by sacrificing innocent animals, she didn't deserve to live. Not in luxury. Not at all.

"Whoa there." Michael placed a firm hand on her shoulder. "She's not out there. She's already been taken into custody and transported back to headquarters."

"Where?" Zuri asked through gritted teeth.

"Whatever you think you're going to do, you're not. You need to calm down."

Was there ever a time in human history when telling someone to *calm down* actually helped the situation?

Zuri could see that Michael also realized the error he had made.

Lucy opened the door and came back into the shop. She let the door close behind her but stayed in front of it.

"She will be punished. Evidence of the gold scheme or not, Lucy witnessed her burning evidence, and she was caught trespassing. She'll also be held accountable for all the animals she sacrificed. They found enough evidence of animal sacrifice to keep her locked up for the rest of her life."

Zuri felt something, no someone, messing with the flow of power surging through her body. It was like a faucet had been turned off. A fire put out. She tried to turn it back on, but she couldn't. A dam blocked the river-like magic that flowed through her. Her access to its current suddenly closed off and unavailable to her.

"I've temporarily sealed off your magic." Lucy crossed her arms over her chest. "The seal will wear off in a day or so. Just long enough for you to regain some of your sense."

"Consider it punishment for coming down here when you were ordered not to," Michael added. Lucy made a face, indicating that she wanted to add a separate punishment for that indiscretion, but she didn't say anything.

"Go home, Zuri," Violet gently commanded.

Lucy stepped aside, clearing a path for Zuri to the door. Without looking back or meeting anyone's eyes, she walked out.

When Zuri pulled up to Claudia's apartment, another car sat in the driveway. A nice car. Zuri didn't know anything about cars, but she could tell this car cost at least her annual salary, maybe more.

Claudia was probably awake. Even if she wasn't, whoever the car belonged to would be. Before getting out of the car, she pulled up a rideshare app and ordered a ride. Two minutes. She needed to grab her laptop and her other things and be outside in two minutes. Without further hesitation, she got out of the car and made her way to the door.

It was unlocked.

"Zuri!" Claudia stood behind the kitchen counter. Her expression was relieved at first, and then hurt and anger took over, knitting her brows together and pulling the corners of her mouth slightly downward.

"How could you—" Julianna started, rising from the couch, but Claudia interrupted her.

"Where's Gigi? Did they find her?"

Zuri started collecting her belongings.

"Zuri!" Julianna yelled.

After stuffing her things into her backpack, Zuri looked at Gigi's bed against the wall. She didn't need it anymore. Maybe Claudia could use it at the clinic, or Julianna could take it to the shelter. She turned back toward the door, her hand paused on the handle.

"Hey!" Julianna threw a cushion at Zuri. It hit the wall next to her head. She didn't even flinch, too tired for Julianna's antics.

"How could you use magic on Claudia!" Julianna continued. "I know you were worried about Gigi, but how could you?"

Zuri turned her head toward Claudia, looking at her, but not really seeing her.

"I'm sorry," she offered. She *was* sorry. It wasn't like she'd planned to do it. It had just happened. In the moment, Claudia had been an obstacle. With her emotions running high, Zuri's magic acted of its own accord to remove any obstacles. There was no question in Zuri's mind that if she could go back in time, she wouldn't change what she did. In fact, she might have done something worse. If only she had gotten there sooner, she might've been able to save Gigi. She was dangerous. Violet was right. She thought she understood that before, with the spoon incident, but it was worse than that. With Gigi gone, there was no need to put Julianna or Claudia in danger anymore.

Her phone dinged. Her ride was there. Without another word, she walked out of the house, down the driveway, and got into the waiting car.

Chapter 23

"Are you trying to blow this place up?" Violet shrieked as she ran over to Zuri, stopping her from pouring a vial ominously labeled *Dragon's Breath* into the cauldron.

"It says to add this." She motioned to the book.

"We don't just *pour* this in! It's extremely volatile. Read the label!" She pointed. In small print, it did indeed say to measure out an eighth of a teaspoon over a sink. *Adding more than 1/8 a teaspoon at a time may lead to fire, explosion, or worse. Use with care.*

Zuri sighed.

"Why do I even need to learn this? It's not like I plan to open a potion shop. When will I use a 'good luck' potion? Especially one that won't work on me." She watched as Violet carefully measured the dragon's fire and added it to their potion.

"Makes a great gift before job interviews, vacations, or when someone is feeling down. You could give it to one of your friends." Violet glanced at her pointedly.

The spot on the floor where she had seen Gigi's remains caught Zuri's attention. Nothing was there anymore. Just empty floor space. She could still picture the skeleton, clean and unnatural looking, though.

"I don't have any friends," she reminded Violet.

"You looked thick as thieves to me. Actually, you were thieves. Even stole something together. You could, I don't know, try talking to them." Violet added the final ingredients to the potion and began to stir.

Zuri shook her head. It was too dangerous. She was too dangerous. She'd been ready to kill Astrid in her grief over losing Gigi. If her emotions got the better of her again, what else could she, would she do, if there was no one around to stop her? No one had been around to stop her from using magic on Claudia. It might not have seemed like such a big deal at first, but at the end of the day, she'd forced Claudia to do something against her will and without her permission. It was wrong.

Hindsight was twenty-twenty. After talking to Violet, she knew any effort to stop Astrid would have been in vain. Even if she had teleported to the shop as soon as Violet's alarm had gone off, she would have been too late. The second the alarm had gone off, Astrid set out to destroy both her Grimoire and Gigi.

It had only been two days since the incident. With the exception of a few angry and demanding texts from Julianna, she hadn't heard from them or tried to reach out.

She was also a little angry with Julianna. How had they even been friends when Julianna wouldn't even explain what she did for a living? It was either wildly lucrative or she was just some trust fund baby, considering the car sitting in the driveway. There was no way she just happened to be borrowing such an expensive car, unless it was from her parents. Whatever the secret was, Claudia clearly also knew and hadn't shared it.

They couldn't trust her, not with intimate details, or with her magic, and she couldn't trust them.

If only she hadn't gone to the shelter and gotten a dog that day, or if only she'd gone to a different shelter. Then she never would have met Julianna or gotten close to Claudia. None of this would have happened.

She was fine with being alone before, but now, without Gigi, without Julianna and Claudia, even with her new mentor, Violet, she felt alone. More alone than she ever had before. It sucked.

"I thought I was supposed to get a letter by owl and get whisked away to magic school. Why am I stuck in your basement?" Zuri flopped down on Violet's amazing black couch. So soft. Her only solace.

"For the last time, it's not a basement. It's my sanctuary," Violet grumbled.

"Sprouts don't go to magic school, not unless their magic arrives at a very early age. They get private tutors, sometimes in small groups. You're stuck with me until a more appropriate mentor can be found, but don't worry, I'll make a witch out of you yet."

"What does that even mean? *More appropriate*," she said mockingly. So far, having magic kind of sucked. It had cost her, her friends and now she had to study. She was supposed to be done with school. She was thirty-one years old. Homework and quizzes were not any more appealing now than they were when she was a kid.

"You've been granted access to a rare and unusual amount of power. We don't even know the full extent yet. You need someone at your level who can teach you how to control it. My power works differently than yours. There's only so much I can teach." Violet turned the cauldron heat down, allowing the potion to simmer.

"It wasn't enough," she whispered. Whatever power she possessed, it wasn't enough to save Gigi. So, what good was it?

Violet bottled her potion and Zuri helped clean up their mess.

"Can't you teach me something useful, like that sleep paralysis spell Astrid used? How can I get out of it if something like that ever happens again?" Zuri dried the measuring spoons and put them back in the correct drawers.

"It won't." Violet sighed as she returned all her ingredient jars and bottles back into the pantry, turning them so the labels faced the front.

"But what if it did? Then what would I do?" She whined.

"It's not complicated." Violet huffed. "It's easy to hold on to something heavy, rigid, and solid. It's more difficult to hold on to something light and fluid, like air or water. Just focus on relaxing. The more relaxed you can make your mind and body, the easier it is to slip out of a holding spell's grasp."

"That sounds like Jedi stuff," she mumbled, but it didn't go unnoticed by Violet.

"Very Jedi indeed." The older witch smiled.

It made sense. Kind of. Like the difference between trying to hold a rock versus water in your hand. The hard part would be being like water. Zuri was definitely more like a rock. Not particularly good at relaxing. Especially on command. She tended to be rigid and tense, even clenching her jaw most nights in her sleep. Hopefully Violet was right, and it wouldn't happen ever again.

Chapter 24

Zuri arrived home from Violet's house a little after 8 p.m. It was still weird coming home without Gigi around. Although their time together had been short, she was used to being greeted at the door now and felt a pang in her heart when she closed the door behind her. It wasn't just Gigi. She'd kind of gotten used to having Claudia or Julianna around, too.

She always thought that she liked, even enjoyed the quiet and solitude of being alone. Her independence was everything to her. Maybe that was only because she hadn't known what it felt like to be in good company in a really long time, if ever. Having other people around was nice, when it was the right people. If only she had learned that sooner.

She sat on the couch and pulled out her phone. She might as well go through her inbox. There were over 100 unread messages. It was very unlike her. Normally, she kept her inbox clutter free, deleting, replying, and saving emails almost as soon as they came in. It was neurotic, but efficient. She had been so focused on Gigi and her new friends that her screen time had significantly dropped. Its usual hold over her, trumped by the mystery of Gigi's enchantment and the company of her friends. She scrolled through the mess, deleting junk mail that had snuck through and opening anything that looked interesting.

It's *puppy season! Get a second GPS collar for your new pup with 20% off.*

GPS collar.

GPS.

She was an idiot. Obviously. Why had she not thought to use the fancy GPS collar when Gigi had gone missing? She'd only bought it because it was pretty, but she had registered it and set everything up. If only she had thought to use it!

Zuri pulled up the app on her phone. It was stupid. There was no sign of the collar at Violet's basement. . . *sanctuary.* It must have been destroyed, like every other part of Gigi, save for her bones.

After what felt like years to load, Zuri stared at the blinking blue dot on her screen. The collar was still active. Not destroyed. Active.

Gigi was alive.

She was alive.

ALIVE!

There was still time to save her. Maybe. *Okay, let's not jump to conclusions,* Zuri reminded herself before taking a deep breath. Just because the collar was active, did not mean Gigi was alive. It could be tied nicely around her corpse. Or maybe the collar had simply been dropped somewhere else to throw off the investigation, only it hadn't worked because Zuri had forgotten all about it.

Studying the location, Zuri mapped it on her phone. It was about an hour away on the outskirts of town. She should call Violet and ask her to contact the investigators and let them check it out. That would be the smart thing to do. The thought of sitting and waiting, however. . . She couldn't do it two nights ago, and she didn't plan on doing it now.

Chapter 25

The option to go alone stood, but she didn't want to go alone, didn't trust herself.

She stared at her phone screen. She needed to hit the call button. There was no time to send a text. If Gigi was still alive, she wouldn't be for much longer. They needed to get her out of there, wherever there was.

She hit the call button and waited.

The phone stopped ringing almost immediately, but instead of a *hello*, Zuri was met with silence on the other end of the line.

"Claudia?" Zuri asked cautiously.

"What do you want, Zuri?" Claudia's no-nonsense, icy tone hit her like an arrow right through the heart.

This was a bad idea. She shouldn't have called, shouldn't have asked Claudia, of all people, for help.

"Say something or I'm hanging up. . ." Claudia sighed, more weariness than annoyance in her voice this time.

Now or never.

"I'm sorry I used my magic on you and made you do something against your will. It was wrong, no matter the circumstances. I didn't really plan it, it just happened. That's not an excuse," she stammered. "I'm just, I'm sorry."

Zuri didn't expect the tears that pricked the back of her eyes. She held back a sniffle.

The line was quiet on the other end.

"The GPS collar. I. . ." she took a deep inhale. "I bought Gigi a GPS collar when I first got her, but I forgot about it. It wasn't destroyed. It's still active. About an hour south." She paused. "I'm going to find it. There's a chance Astrid lied. Gigi might be there."

Dead air. Claudia said nothing, but she didn't hang up either. Maybe it would have been easier if she had. If she told Zuri that she didn't want anything to do with her anymore, that would be it. It would hurt more to hear her say it than to assume it, but it was better than silence. Her bottom lip began to quiver. She didn't have time for these emotions. Gigi could be out of time at any moment, if she was even still alive.

"Okay, well—"

"Are you asking me to go with you?" Claudia cut her off. She sounded exasperated and Zuri didn't blame her.

This was a bad idea. The veil of dread that already hung over her head shrouded her body. A rock sat on her chest.

"Yeah," she almost whispered. "Only if you want to."

"Zuri. . ." Claudia sighed.

"I just thought. . ." She trailed off. "I don't know what I was thinking. I'm sorry."

She was pathetic. Of course Claudia wouldn't want to go. There was a zero percent chance. It had been a bad idea to call. Honestly, if the situation was reversed, she probably, no, she definitely wouldn't have answered. She pulled the phone away from her ear.

"Wait!" Claudia yelled before she could end the call.

She put the phone to her ear again.

"I'll pick you up. I'll be there in fifteen minutes." Claudia sounded like she couldn't believe she was agreeing to this any more than Zuri could, but she would take it.

"Thanks."

Claudia hung up without warning.

Now she had to try Julianna. Her mind flashed back to Julianna's angry, scowling face the last time she'd seen her. If, and only if, Julianna answered the phone, she was going to get an earful rather than icy silence. Oh boy.

She dialed. It rang. And rang. And rang. The voicemail wasn't even set up. That was so Julianna.

A text would have to do. It was possible Claudia would also give Julianna a call. Maybe they were talking now.

I'm sorry, she started to type but stopped. She *was* sorry. Sorry their new friendship had abruptly ended. While Zuri had kind of been the one to walk away first, it wasn't necessarily entirely her fault. She hadn't done anything to Julianna, except shut her out. To be fair, it wasn't like Julianna had ever even let her in. She understood why Julianna was mad. It was not okay what she'd done to Claudia, but she only owed Claudia an apology for that.

Zuri deleted the message and instead sent the address for where they were going and their ETA. If Julianna wanted to join them, that would be her choice.

Her phone pinged. A reply from Julianna already. Instead of a text, it was a voice note. Wearily, Zuri hit play.

"Dishonor on you! Dishonor on your whole family! Except Gigi because she deserves better—" Zuri hit pause and closed her messages. Yikes. She was still mad. Really mad. It didn't sound like she was ready to talk. It was unlikely she would be joining them. Probably for the best. After all, Zuri didn't even know what they were going to find there.

She stood and ducked her head inside her shirt, wiping away the remaining tears. Hopefully, they would only find Gigi. Alive. She would be alive. They had to. Anything else was unthinkable. Grabbing the forget-me stick from her room just in case, she went outside to wait for Claudia.

Awkward wasn't a strong enough word for the car ride over to the GPS's coordinates. Zuri got in the car, but Claudia didn't even look at her before pulling out of her driveway. Neither one of them spoke for the first half of the drive. Gone was their easy and comfortable atmosphere.

"Thanks, for driving." Zuri decided to speak first. Claudia didn't answer.

"I'm sorry, again, for before." Silence.

"I'm not sure what we're going to find when we get there," she continued. "Um. . . it might be dangerous."

Claudia snorted.

It was another ten minutes before either of them spoke again.

"I'm mad at you." Claudia's knuckles turned white as she gripped the steering wheel.

"I messed up. I'm sorry." She felt herself shrinking in her seat.

"I know you're sorry, but I'm still mad at you." Claudia took her eyes off the road for a second to glare at her.

"I never once, not once. . ." Claudia paused. "After Violet told us about magic, about your powers, *not once* did I think you'd ever use them on me. I know you just put me to sleep, but you didn't know what you were doing. Remember the spoon? What if the magic hadn't worn off? What if I never woke up again?"

Everything she said was right. Zuri didn't have an excuse, so she didn't say anything.

"And you stole my car! I didn't even know you and I let you stay at my house, and you stole my car. I broke into a witch's basement for you!" Claudia continued.

Trust, broken. Her shoulders inched toward her ears as she sunk even further into her seat. If only it would swallow her.

One thing was still bothering Zuri. It didn't make sense. If she was still so angry, why did she even answer the phone? Julianna hadn't. There was no reason for her to be there. This was and had always been Zuri's problem. No one else was responsible for Gigi.

"Why are you here?"

Claudia didn't answer right away. She felt sorry for anything in Claudia's line of sight. She could start a fire with the glare she was giving the road right then.

A few minutes later, Claudia pulled over. Zuri briefly began to panic that she was going to kick her out of the car. There was no way she would be able to catch a ride out there, especially not this late.

Once the car had stopped, Claudia put it in park and turned to look at her. She tried not to squirm under her gaze.

"I'm mad at you, but I'm still your friend. So, when you call me telling me you're going to drive to some shady commercial property at the edge of town to find Gigi's collar, of course, I'm not going to let you go alone."

A wave of relief washed over Zuri, and she couldn't help the tears that fell.

"You're a really ugly crier." Claudia snorted. "There are some napkins in the glove box."

"Thanks." She sniffed, reaching for the napkins.

"Julianna's going to meet us there. She called me when I left to pick you up." Claudia pulled back onto the road and got them back on course. Zuri spent the rest of the ride trying to get herself together.

They soon pulled up near the coordinates of Gigi's collar. There really was nothing out there. Just a single manufactured building, surrounded by a crude and old-looking wooden fence. A black SUV was parked next to the building, along with a white sedan. Claudia parked farther away from the building, on the side of a small dirt road, just to be safe. There wasn't much to shield them from the building's view, but at least no one would hear the car pulling up.

Only a few minutes later, Julianna parked behind them in the same expensive-looking black sedan that had been in Claudia's driveway.

Zuri and Claudia got out of the car and closed their doors as quietly as possible. There wasn't much around to stop the sound from traveling to the building. Julianna got out of her car, but upon seeing Zuri, slammed her door and crossed her arms over her chest.

"Jules!" Claudia scolded her in a loud whisper. "The goal is stealth."

Julianna lifted her chin defiantly before shooting Zuri a glare. Oh, she could play this game too. Leaning the forget-me stick on the car door, she looked at Julianna's car and back at her, crossing her arms over her chest too, mirroring the other woman's stance.

"Can you two cut it out? We don't know what we're up against and it would be best if we did this as a team, not as enemies." Claudia rolled her eyes.

"I'm only here for Gigi." Julianna sniffed.

Claudia groaned.

Zuri pulled out her phone. She sent Violet a text with their location, what they were doing, and that she may want to call the investigators over, just in case. If things didn't go well, she wanted at least one person to know what happened.

She didn't expect an immediate response, but only a few seconds after sending the text, her phone started ringing, the name *Violet* big on her screen. Uh-oh.

Instead of answering, she turned her phone off. Technically, no one had told her this was the Witch's Council's business. As far as she knew, their investigation was over. Even if she got in trouble, it would be worth it.

"All good?" Claudia bumped her shoulder. Zuri almost dropped her phone.

"Yeah, backup should be on the way, just in case." She nodded.

"Good. Now let's get down to business to defeat whatever witch stole Gigi." Julianna punched her left palm with her right hand.

"Can you please stop quoting Mulan?" Zuri hissed. All the songs were going to be stuck in her head for the rest of the night if she kept it up.

"Think you can make us invisible?" Claudia turned toward the building and started walking.

She froze.

"I was just joking," Claudia whispered over her shoulder. Right. Of course. Zuri forced her limbs back into motion again.

They made the short walk to the building and crouched below the windows. Luckily, it was dark, and no one seemed to be outside.

Zuri peeked through the window first. On the opposite wall, someone had stacked kennels on top of each other haphazardly, some of them containing animals. She looked to the right. More kennels pushed against the wall, barely leaving enough room for a door. To the left, in a single kennel, was Gigi, her overpriced pink floral collar still around her neck. Any buyer's remorse she previously felt for the collar evaporated.

"I see her!" Zuri whispered, maybe a little too loud. She ducked back down.

"And we see you," a familiar female voice sounded from the side of the building, startling Zuri. The forget-me stick clattered to the ground.

Dr. Rachel Smith. But if Rachel had Gigi, then that meant...

"You and Astrid were working together the entire time." Claudia stood, glaring at Rachel and the fake animal control officer who walked up behind her.

Julianna and Zuri stood, and Zuri stepped slightly in front of them.

"The ring. From my dream. It was hers, not Astrid's." Zuri shook her head, noticing, not for the first time, the red ruby ring on Rachel's hand. She hadn't known what it was the first time she had seen it. Of course everything was clicking into place now that it was too late.

"We're just here for Gigi. Give her to us and we can all pretend we were never here." Zuri didn't want to leave the other animals, but Gigi took priority over the others. Besides, backup was already on the way. The Witch's Council could save the other victims.

"I'm afraid you've seen too much. You'll be staying, indefinitely." *Ugh*. How cliché.

"The strays people bring in. You always claimed the owner came in for them. Have you been taking them and casting that horrible spell on them with Astrid this entire time?" Claudia asked.

"You think you're so smart, Dr. Perfect." Rachel rolled her eyes. "Duh. They might as well be good for something."

"Are the animals inside already enchanted?" Zuri asked. A plan was forming in her mind.

"No, Astrid was supposed to—"

"Rich!" Rachel cut the man, *Rich*, off. "Less yapping. Tie them up."

"With what?" He looked around.

Before they could figure it out, Zuri took a deep breath. She felt her magic in her veins and beneath her skin. She was ready. Her plan would work. It seemed like the more she let the magic do what it wanted, the easier it was. It had a mind of its own, as if it were alive. Separate, but part of her. So, instead of trying to control, she simply let it flow.

Above them, the windows slid open, and on the other side of the building, the door swung open too. All the doors for the animal cages opened at once, causing chaos as dozens of animals fled from the windows and doors.

"RUN!" she yelled to Julianna and Zuri, as Rachel and Rich stared in horror at the chaos. She scanned the fleeing animals but didn't see Gigi.

She turned and saw that her friends had taken off, Claudia in the lead and Julianna not far behind her. Instead of following them, Zuri ran around the building and in through the door. The room in the entryway appeared to be some kind of makeshift office. She strode through it, to the door near the side of the building where she had seen Gigi. Gigi was still in the kennel. The door was open, but she didn't move.

She got closer and stooped down. Gigi gave a small whine of acknowledgement but didn't lift her head. Zuri ran her hands through Gigi's fur and brought her forehead down to Gigi's. A wave of relief washed over her, but a sinking feeling of dread quickly replaced it.

There wasn't much time left, that she was certain of. If the dog had any energy to walk, she would've fled with the other animals. There was no time to wait for Violet to figure out the proper way to reverse the spell. Gigi would die soon if she didn't try. She could feel her magic again, reaching toward Gigi. It wanted to fix this, so she let it. Moving her hands in front of Gigi and holding them there as if she was warming them by a fire. She closed her eyes and let the magic do what it wanted.

She saw it. Not with her eyes, but a new way of seeing, a sixth sense. The spell was like a tightly woven net, binding and trapping Gigi. Her magic flowed through it and snapped the strands one by one until, finally, the entire net disintegrated. Gigi was free.

Before she could get her out of the kennel, she heard a large shriek behind her. She turned. Astrid stood in the doorway with her fists clenched at her sides.

"What did you do!" Astrid screamed before she extended a hand toward Zuri without letting her answer.

Honestly, she looked a little like Darth Vader about to force choke someone. If she wasn't about to be on the receiving end, Zuri probably would have laughed. Instead, she felt the invisible force of Astrid's magic grab her as if she was being tied up.

She couldn't move her arms or legs. For a moment, she could barely breathe, but as the witch's focus shifted to Gigi, her grip on Zuri softened, allowing her to take a full breath. She pushed against the invisible binds, but they refused to loosen anymore. Not even an inch.

Astrid went to the kennel, and the black Chow greeted her with a snarl. Her white teeth glinted in warning. The witch slammed the kennel door in Gigi's face.

It looked like the dog was feeling at least a little better now that the spell was broken. She still needed to eat, but hopefully she would make a full recovery with time. That allowed Zuri to relax a little. As her shoulders relaxed and her muscles loosened, she felt Astrid's hold on her begin to slip as she stopped fighting it. Violet was right. If she could just find a way to relax, she could still get them out of this.

Rachel strode into the room, sweat dripping down the side of her face.

"Did you get the other two?" Astrid turned to Rachel.

"They split up, and with all the animals loose, it was impossible to pursue them on foot. Rich is going after them in his car now."

Zuri could see blood dripping down Rachel's left leg. A nasty bite wound gaped open on her thigh.

She deserved it and more, as far as Zuri was concerned. It was also just a dumb move to wear shorts in this kind of working environment. As a vet, she should have known better.

The other witch caught Zuri eyeing her wound, and she sneered.

"Aren't you supposed to be in jail or something?" That's what the investigators had said. There was supposed to be enough evidence, with or without the Grimoire or Gigi.

"I have an excellent lawyer," Astrid smiled as if she'd read Zuri's mind. Surprise, surprise. The witch justice system was no better than the human one. Awesome.

"We should get out of here. The council's special investigators are probably already on the way." Rachel took a step toward the windows and peered outside. "Let's get the dog and go."

"The dog's useless now." Astrid scowled again.

"What? How?" Rachel looked at Gigi and Zuri could see it on her face when she realized the spell was broken and Gigi was no longer enchanted.

"Did Violet reverse engineer my potion? I never could figure out a way to reverse it. Would make hiding the evidence a lot easier. Could use the same animal more than once instead of having to get a bunch."

Zuri could see the older witch doing the calculations in her head. She didn't answer. Instead, she took another breath and tried to relax again. The longer they stayed here talking, the better the chance of help arriving before any harm could come to her or Gigi and before the ones responsible for all of this could get away. Everything was going to be fine. Astrid wouldn't get away with it this time, no matter how great her lawyer was.

"Astrid, we need to leave," Rachel said again. "Let's get rid of the girl and the dog and go."

Zuri took a final deep breath in and a long slow exhale out. She opened her mouth to stop clenching her jaw, released the tension in her back, and felt the ground under her feet. As soon as she felt the weight of Astrid's bind release, she didn't hesitate. Just like before, she could feel her magic, her power, ready to act, and she unleashed it onto the two witches without a second thought.

They both flew out the windows with a loud crash, shattering the glass.

"If I'd known you could do that, I would have been nicer to you when we got here."

Zuri turned and found Julianna and Claudia in the doorway.

"I told you to run!" She yelled at them.

"We did, back toward the cars and then—" Claudia started.

"Later! Let's get Gigi and go." She rushed toward the kennel, Claudia and Julianna behind her. Claudia, the strongest of the three, lifted poor Gigi out of the kennel. Nowhere near her ideal weight, Claudia carried her out the door and out of the building with ease.

They didn't get far before she felt Astrid's magic reach for them, but this time she was ready. Well, her magic was ready. She turned, and it blocked the attempted hold, with no input from her whatsoever. Later, she would probably freakout about this weird symbiotic thing they had going on. Now she needed to stay focused on getting away. The two witches had caught up and weren't going to let them leave without a fight.

Claudia handed Gigi to Julianna and nodded at her to keep going to the car, now parked only a few yards away. With no hesitation, she lunged at Rachel, punching her right in the face. The witch went down, and before she could get back up, Claudia kicked her in the stomach, offering no mercy. She was not kidding when she said she knew how to fight.

"How dare you call yourself a veterinarian!" She kicked Rachel again, but the witch pointed her ringed finger at Claudia, flinging her backward and to the ground.

Before Zuri could help her, Astrid tried to hold her again, and Zuri's attention was drawn to her own magic blocking the attack.

"Well, well." Astrid stepped closer. "You've ruined my plans, and my life. I think it's only fair that I ruin yours."

Zuri heard Claudia scream, but her eyes stayed trained on Astrid's hand as it waved toward Claudia's car. The vehicle floated off the ground, several stories above them.

"I do want to know one thing, though." Astrid spun the car in a little circle. Zuri looked up and realized Julianna wasn't inside. Okay. That was good. They were safe. For now.

"How did you break the spell on the dog?" Astrid stared at her as if she could find the answer on Zuri's face.

She shrugged and she could see from the fire in Astrid's eyes that she found her nonchalance infuriating.

"TELL ME!" Astrid lifted the car higher.

"I didn't do anything special." Zuri looked at the car, at least three stories off the ground by now. It was moving closer to where Rachel stood, holding Claudia suspended in a bone crushing bind only a few feet away from her.

Movement behind Astrid from the doorway of the building caught Zuri's eye. Julianna. It had to be.

"I just reached for it with my magic and broke the threads," Zuri continued, focusing her gaze back on Astrid.

"Broke the threads? What kind of garbage is that?" Astrid continued moving the car. It was on top of Rachel and Claudia now. Not good.

"Yeah, the magic was woven around Gigi like a net. I used my magic to cut each thread until it was enough to release her." Astrid looked incredulous, but Zuri kept her focus on Julianna and what looked like a glimmer of something shiny in the doorway's shadow. She looked at Claudia and Rachel again. Claudia met her gaze, her mouth a tight line as blood trickled out of her nose.

"Well, this has been lovely, but I think it's time we get home," Zuri stated, and as soon as she saw Julianna come out of the house behind Astrid with the forget-me stick in her hands, she leapt toward Claudia, pushing her out from under the car.

The bat connected with Astrid's skull, causing the car to fall right on top of Rachel, only twelve inches from where Claudia and Zuri lay on the ground.

"Are you okay?" Zuri had wrapped her arms around Claudia as they fell, cradling her head to keep it from making impact with the ground.

"Might be better if you got off me." A winded Claudia took a deep breath in. Zuri rolled off her. But she wasn't ready to stand up yet, hoping that a bat to the head had at least put Astrid out for a few minutes, if not forever. The adrenaline of the night was catching up with her and her hands started shaking.

Claudia stayed on the ground beside her and reached for her hand, interlacing their fingers.

"That was a little too close." Claudia tightened her grip on Zuri's hand.

"If you get another cat, I promise to risk my life to save it. If you know, a witch ever casts a spell on it."

"I definitely won't be getting any more pets from Tails, that's for sure."

"I heard that!" Julianna yelled.

The sound of tires squealing caused Zuri to spring to her feet and away from Claudia as three black SUVs drove toward them rapidly. She took up a fighting stance but relaxed as the cars stopped and Violet jumped out of one, followed by Michael, Lucy, and several others whom Zuri didn't recognize.

The newcomers stared at the scene, some with jaws reaching down to the ground.

"So, should we call an ambulance, or can you heal with magic?" Zuri was met with blank stares. She walked over to Gigi, who was still weak but at least no longer enchanted. The dog was panting, her blue-black tongue hanging out of her mouth, but she smiled up at Zuri.

"Well, Claudia and Gigi could use some help if you have a healer. And I guess these two." Zuri gestured to Astrid, who laid unconscious on the ground nearby, and to Rachel, who was very quiet underneath the car.

"Oh yeah, and the third guy. Rich." Claudia looked toward the road, a little more blood dripping from her nose onto the ground.

"His car crashed over there," Julianna pointed.

Again, they were met with silence for a full beat until Michael started barking orders. After that, people got to work. At least a dozen witches either assisted the injured, caught the loose animals or gathered evidence from the crime scene.

"What happened?" Violet rushed over to where they stood near the building. Zuri watched as a few witches helped Astrid and Rachel. Neither moved on their own. They remained still, their eyes closed.

"It's a long story." Zuri sighed.

Chapter 26

Zuri insisted on taking Gigi back to her place before she would give Lucy and Michael her statement about the events. They weren't happy about her demand, but they also couldn't force her to talk.

She sat on the floor next to Gigi's dog bed, absently stroking her back as she relayed the events of the evening. Gigi remained lethargic, but before they'd left the scene, a witch whose job was to heal at magical crime and accident scenes ensured she was in good shape and that there would be no lasting damage from the spell. Gigi had growled at the woman at first, but with Zuri holding her, she let the woman do her work. Finally, back at home, she was doing much better after some chicken and rice, which Julianna whipped up for her in no time.

Lucy and Michael got updates from the scene and shared some of the information with them. It turned out Rachel had enough time to at least shield herself from some of the car's impact. The sudden surge of magic and the remaining force of the car had knocked her out, but she would make a full recovery. Eventually.

Astrid apparently had a harder head than most people. The blow had cracked her skull but she wouldn't have any lasting damage. Thanks to the help of some magic healers, she would also make a full recovery. They would live to pay for their crimes, and Zuri wouldn't have it any other way. If the Witch's Council was to be as feared as Violet made them out to be, maybe the pair would have to suffer the same fate as the animals they'd tortured. She could only hope.

Rich, or *fake animal control officer*, as she'd gotten used to referring to him as, turned out not to even be a witch. Astrid enchanted the man, not with magic, but with promises of riches. She needed an expendable human to do some of her more labor-intensive bidding, and Rich hadn't been hard to convince.

The investigators arrested him too, to be tried as well. Zuri didn't see how they could hold him accountable to laws he possibly hadn't known about as a non-magical person, but Claudia reminded her that ignorance of a law doesn't mean you could break it. She had a point. If someone drove and didn't know red meant stop, it didn't mean they wouldn't get a ticket if they didn't.

Upon telling the investigators about how she broke the spell on Gigi and the little magic she'd used during their scuffle, she got worried. They kept sharing knowing glances. Their shoulders stiffened and the corners of their mouths drooped down as they listened.

"You're saying you can *see* magic?" Lucy asked slowly.

"No, I mean, not all the time. Not with my eyes. I don't know how to explain it. I was seeing it, the threads of the spell on Gigi. But not seeing. Feeling it." She bit her lip. She wasn't making any sense, even to herself.

"And your magic. How did you figure out what to do to break the spell, to control it so quickly?" Michael asked casually, but Zuri could see a deep interest in his eyes.

"I just wanted it, and I felt my magic want to do it, so I let it. It's not about control, it's about letting go. Is that not how it's supposed to work? That's how Violet had me break the wards on Astrid's Grimoire." Zuri looked toward Violet, who had been slowly tiptoeing toward the door.

"You knew, the whole time?" Lucy crossed her arms over her chest and looked at Violet accusingly.

Violet heaved a sigh and turned back around.

"Knew what?" Zuri looked between them.

"I suspected, but didn't know anything for sure." Violet moved away from the door and sat down on Zuri's couch, but she refused to make eye contact.

"You're no sprout." Michael put his head in his hands, exasperated. This was not looking good.

"But I have to be, right? I don't come from a magical family." Zuri stopped petting Gigi and stood up.

"There have been some powerful sprouts in the past, but what you just described. . ." He trailed off.

"There are only a few lines of magic capable of wielding and interacting with it the way you can," Violet nearly whispered.

"Zuri. . . Hansen, was it?" Lucy tilted her head, considering. "What about your mother? What's her maiden name?"

Zuri snorted.

"Hansen. That's her maiden name."

"Your parents aren't married?" Michael asked in more of a curious than accusing way.

"Oh, my mother's been married alright. About seven times. At least. I've lost track. She gave me her maiden name as my last name." Zuri shrugged. She didn't enjoy talking about her family, especially her mother. She hadn't even told Claudia or Julianna about her family yet. Julianna would definitely ask her for details later. Zuri could feel her curious eyes on her without even glancing over.

"And your father's last name?" Lucy gave her an intense gaze that made her feel like she could see inside Zuri's head.

"Blackhammer."

Michael abruptly stood and moved away from her. Lucy joined him. Zuri turned to Violet. The woman's eyes were wide with terror.

"Blackhammer is your father?" Lucy's voice became icy.

"Your father is indeed a powerful warlock." Michael sighed.

"Extremely powerful," Lucy added, a grave look on her face.

"But. . . that's not possible." Zuri shook her head.

Michael waved his hands, and a holographic image of a wanted poster floated in front of Zuri.

None of them recognized it at first, recognized *her* at first, but they must have seen it then. The man in the photo was darker than her, his head clean-shaven. His dark eyes filled with anger that pierced whoever or whatever he was looking at. The man was a stranger to her, but shared similar eyes, high cheekbones, and even now. . . She clenched her jaw.

"That's him, isn't it?" Michael asked, his voice becoming harder, stony.

"That's not my dad." Zuri blinked.

It was true. While the man in the holograph looked similar, she knew her father had a scar above his right eyebrow. A childhood bike accident. Her father had also been slimmer, less muscular.

"You share some features with this man. Are you sure?" Lucy asked.

They were probably related, but he wasn't her father. It had been years, over two decades, but she was sure this wasn't him.

"David Blackhammer," Zuri read from the holograph. "I don't remember my dad's family, if he had any siblings, but I know his first name isn't David. It's Malik."

"David has a younger brother, doesn't he?" Michael asked Lucy.

"I believe he does. This must be her uncle. The brother had his powers sealed away decades ago, as a boy," Lucy answered.

"When was the last time you saw your father?" Michael swept the image away as quickly as he'd brought it up.

"Not since I was in elementary school. It's been at least twenty years," Zuri mumbled.

This wasn't good. They were looking at her like she'd done something wrong.

"She's telling the truth." Lucy nodded, and she saw Michael's shoulders relax a little.

"He doesn't know. He can't know?" Violet was speaking to no one in particular, but Lucy and Michael nodded.

"Doesn't know what?" Claudia ventured.

"About Zuri's magic. If he did, Blackhammer would have come for her." Michael shook his head. "He can't find out. At least not yet." The two investigators strode toward the door.

"Violet, keep an eye on her. If anything, and I mean *anything*, comes up, call us." Michael opened the door.

Violet nodded, her lips pursed and eyes .

"Wait! Where are you going?" Zuri called.

"We're going to make sure no one finds out about your real identity. Blackhammer cannot get wind of this," Michael barely explained before rushing out the door, slamming it behind him.

"This isn't over, is it?" Claudia turned to Violet.

"No dear, I'd say it's only the beginning." She sighed.

"What exactly did my uncle do? And why was my dad's magic sealed away?" Zuri asked.

"Your uncle believes we should be able to do whatever we want with our magic. Doesn't like rules. He encourages other witches and warlocks to break them," Violet summarized.

"To do things like what Astrid did to Gigi?" Zuri asked.

"More or less, but on a bigger scale. To use magic not just for personal gain, but to take power, even over entire countries. He believes those with the strongest magic have a right to use it to take whatever they can," Violet explained.

"And my dad" Zuri asked.

"When someone repeatedly breaks the law and tries to disrupt the order of things, the Council sometimes seals away their magic. To make sure the family doesn't retaliate or try to break the seal, the Council sometimes seals the entire family's magic."

"That seems kind of harsh." Julianna jumped to sit on top of the kitchen island.

"The sentencing wasn't decided on a whim. It was created after multiple families tried to unseal a convicted witch's magic and after council members were injured in retaliation." Violet started moving toward the door. "In your case Zuri, your uncle escaped before sentencing, so the council sealed the Blackhammer family magic and intends to finish the job when your uncle is caught again. If he's caught again. It's been decades, but the Council still hasn't been able to bring him in."

"So, he's still out there? Doing what exactly?" Zuri bit the inside of her cheek. Her uncle was a wanted criminal of the supervillain variety. Great. Hopefully, she would never meet him. She hadn't really been interested in reconnecting with her dad's side of the family before, and now she definitely wasn't.

"There's a rumor he was involved in the recent theft of a magical amulet on display at the Museum of Magic, but I don't know much else. I don't much care about politics or bad news."

"Does that mean that they'll seal my magic like my dad's? Because of my uncle?" Zuri asked. She shivered, her magic vibrating beneath her skin.

Violet pursed her lips again, and like the day they met her at the shop, looked off into the distance as if she were talking to someone else. She suddenly shrugged.

"This is a highly unusual case. With your father's magic sealed before you were even born, it shouldn't have been passed down to you. Especially since your mother doesn't have magic at all. We don't even know what unlocked your magic to begin with. I have no idea how the Witch's Council will react."

Zuri felt her chest tighten. Uncertainty. She didn't like it. It would be easier if Violet or Michael and Lucy could tell her exactly what was going to happen. After everything she had just been through to find and rescue Gigi, she needed to know things were going to go back to normal. Or at least closer to normal. She looked at Claudia and Julianna. Their expressions mirrored how she was feeling. It wasn't reassuring.

"It's late. Or early, depending on how you look at it. I should get home. I'll check in with you tomorrow." Violet let herself out.

"I'm going to head out too." Julianna hopped off the island. "And I'm still mad at you!" She pointed at Zuri and gave her the stink eye.

"Thanks. For everything." Zuri stood and followed her to the door.

"You're the worst kind of person to be mad at." Julianna suddenly enveloped her into a hug before practically running out the door.

Zuri watched her glide down the sidewalk to her ridiculously fancy car. Car. Claudia's car was trashed. She turned.

Claudia still sat on the sofa, watching her.

"I'm sorry about your car. We can see if Violet can fix it after the investigation is over." Zuri crossed her arms over her chest and rocked from one foot to the other.

"It wasn't your fault, but yeah, not sure my insurance will cover magic related disasters." Claudia stood.

"Do you want a ride?"

"Sure."

Chapter 27

They drove the short distance to Claudia's house in near silence. Gigi laid in the back seat snoring softly. Zuri should have let her rest at home, but she wasn't ready to let her dog out of her sight again, not yet.

"Can I ask you something?" Claudia turned to face Zuri as they pulled into her driveway.

"Sure." She put the car in park and turned to face her. Despite everything, or maybe because of everything, it was still hard for Zuri to look her in the eyes. She focused on the bridge of her nose instead.

"What does it feel like when you use magic?"

The wheels in Zuri's head stopped turning for a moment. She wasn't expecting that kind of question.

"It feels like," she paused and thought about it, "like just wanting something and asking for it to happen. Like, the magic is alive and self-aware and wants to help me. It's kind of hard to explain. Maybe it's a little like Genie from *Aladdin*, but a lot less talkative."

"Will you miss it? If they take it away?" Claudia unbuckled her seat belt.

Would she? It wasn't like she even knew what to do with it, not really. A less anxious version of herself would probably be excited about it, but if she was honest, she still feared it. She remembered her fury when she had thought Astrid had killed Gigi and about how easy it had been to use magic on Claudia. The magic took over, guided by her raw emotions. Corrupted by them to do terrible things on her behalf. If she kept it, she might seriously hurt someone. While the excited childlike part of herself still wondered what she could do with magic or how it might make life easier, the fear she felt outweighed any potential benefits.

Most people probably wouldn't understand, but her brain was wired differently. Fear almost always won. She wasn't proud of it, but it was just how things were. Maybe one day it would be different. She could be different. Rescuing Gigi had proved that she could be brave when she needed to be. But she had lived thirty-one years without magic and she could easily keep living without it now.

If she kept the magic, everything would get turned upside down. Her entire life would change, and not all for the better. It would definitely drive a wedge between her and her friends. It already had. She just wanted a cozy home with her sweet, now unenchanted, dog. She also wanted her friendship with Julianna to continue, despite her secrets and their fight. And Claudia. She wanted Claudia too. More than she should, especially after using magic on her.

With Gigi disenchanted, they didn't really have a reason to keep seeing each other. Not unless Claudia wanted to.

"I won't miss the magic." She took Claudia's hand in her own, lacing their fingers together. "But I will miss you."

"I'm not going anywhere." Claudia leaned over, her face inches from Zuri, but she waited for Zuri to close the gap between them.

Zuri, the introvert that she was, hadn't kissed anyone in an embarrassingly long time, but her body still remembered. For once, she didn't hesitate. The wheels spinning in her head stopped as her mouth melted with Claudia's. For once, her mind was quiet. No thinking necessary. She tried to get closer, but realized the seatbelt was holding her back. Claudia unbuckled it for her and pulled Zuri toward her until she was practically sitting in her lap.

Kissing Claudia was definitely better than having all the magic in the world.

Chapter 28

Wednesday

Zuri stood in the center of a dark room that reminded her of a courtroom. The walls were a dark oak and swirls of crown molding connected them to a glass ceiling that let in the light from the night sky. The moon and stars shined brighter here, their rays of light reaching down to bless the earth.

Instead of a single judge, she faced twelve, all hiding their eyes and bodies in dark, heavy cloaks and hoods. Floating candles illuminated their phantomlike figures from behind. They surrounded her, as if they thought she might run away, never mind that she had walked into the room of her own free will.

She wasn't facing them alone. Michael, Lucy, and Violet stood just outside the circle of witches and warlocks who were about to decide her fate. They waited by the door quietly. Violet's mouth sat in a hard line and Zuri saw her wipe a tear from her cheek. For someone like Violet who had known magic her whole life, the chance of it being taken away was worse than death. She had even tried to persuade Michael and Lucy to postpone the meeting with the council, but their hands were tied.

"The law is clear. The families of career criminals like Blackhammer are to have their magic sealed," a hooded man to Zuri's right declared.

"But she didn't have her magic until recently and has no real relationship with her uncle or father," a tall, hooded woman to Zuri's left argued.

"Besides, Malik Blackhammer was only a teenager when David began his violent campaign to seize power. There's no need to punish his offspring. The other members of the Blackhammer family have been punished enough," a third hooded person in front of Zuri said.

"If her magic was triggered and the seal on the family broken, isn't that a sign that we should leave her be?" a fourth spoke up.

"What do you think will happen when he finds out about her magic?" the first man asked.

"He targets powerful witches and wizards, corrupts them. Is she equipped to go against such power?" a fifth council member questioned.

"If we leave her be, she may wind up dead, her blood on our hands," a sixth council member spoke.

Zuri listened to them argue about what to do with her. They spoke about her like she wasn't there.

It was her life they were discussing, but no one bothered to ask her opinion. They all assumed the magic was important to her, that she wanted it. They were wrong.

At thirty-one years old, she had lived her entire life without magic. Over the last couple of weeks, her encounters with it had mostly led to trouble. Gigi was cured of her curse. The last thing she needed was more witches or warlocks coming into her life. It might have been fine before when she was alone, but she wasn't alone now. She had people who were close to her, real friends. If keeping her magic might put them in danger again, or if it increased the chance that her uncle would come for her, Zuri didn't need it.

Her magic vibrated beneath her skin and through her veins, the feeling pleasant and soothing, almost intoxicating. It wanted to stay free, to stay part of her.

Zuri shook off the feeling, and her magic retreated, giving her room to think clearly again. It was too dangerous. She wasn't a risk-taker. It had to go.

"You can seal my magic, or whatever," Zuri interrupted them.

They stared at her, not expecting her to contribute to the conversation at all, and definitely not like that. From the way Michael, Lucy, and Violet had acted after the Council summons, she knew having one's magic sealed away was something most witches and warlocks would try to avoid at all costs. But she wasn't a witch. Not really. And she had never been someone who craved power either. All she really wanted was to be at home with Gigi, relaxing on her sofa with a book, a good blanket, and a hot mug of tea. No more adventures. No more basement sanctuaries. No more cauldrons.

"If we seal your magic, it's nearly irreversible. You won't be able to change your mind," the first man said.

"I don't need magic. I just wanted to disenchant my dog. If what you're saying about my uncle coming to find me is true, I'd rather you just take my magic now." Zuri looked to her right at the first council member, the one who seemed to be in charge. The hood of his cloak hid his eyes, but his mouth sat in a line of displeasure.

"Your opinion on your fate has been noted." He addressed the other eleven members of the Council. "Enough discussion, let us vote. All in favor of sealing her magic away?"

Eight of the witches and warlocks around her proclaimed, "Aye," including the man leading the others through the proceedings. The other four stood silent, waves of disappointment rolling off them.

"It has been decided. Your magic will be sealed." He nodded. "But we will have to keep watch over you. It is unclear what Blackhammer already knows."

"This isn't going to hurt, is it?" Zuri took a step back, suddenly very nervous. Why hadn't she thought about that sooner?

"You shouldn't feel a thing." The man smiled before raising his hands toward the sky, the other council members joining him. They began chanting in unison and blinding white light radiated from their hands. Zuri covered her eyes, but she shouldn't have bothered. The council members brought their hands down in front of them, aiming the light at her. *Liar*, she thought before the intense pain that flowed from the crown of her head to each of her toes caused her to lose consciousness.

Chapter 29

Saturday

"I will never forgive them for this!" Julianna yelled before falling back onto the sofa, bowl of popcorn in both hands.

"It was my decision to have my magic sealed, Julianna." Zuri sighed. Over the past few days, she had thought about it, and so far she couldn't say that she regretted her decision.

"Then I'll never forgive *you*." Julianna threw a handful of popcorn at her face.

"I don't know why you invited her." Claudia set three steaming mugs of spicy herbal chai tea down on the coffee table before taking the middle seat between them.

"I didn't know you were going to be here either. No lovey-dovey PDA, okay? As happy as I am that you two FINALLY got together, I don't need to see that." Julianna threw popcorn in Claudia's face.

"What do you mean, *finally*? We've only known each other a couple of weeks." Claudia glared at Julianna and grabbed the bowl, passing it to Zuri.

"Could have been a thing from day one." Julianna tried to reach for the bowl again, but Claudia slapped her hand away.

"Can you *please* finally tell me what your secret job is and why the shelter hasn't put in a restraining order against you for giving away animals?" Zuri pleaded.

"She sells feet pictures." Claudia smirked.

"You PROMISED you wouldn't tell anyone!" Julianna screamed, leaping off the couch and pointing a finger at Claudia accusingly.

"She made so much money selling feet pictures that she makes these huge donations to the shelter. They can't afford to make her angry." Claudia shoved a handful of popcorn into her mouth, satisfied.

"I *used* to sell feet pictures. That's how I got my seed money. Now my money comes from my investments into the pet industry. Did you know that even when there's a recession, people still keep spending on their pets?" She flopped back down.

"Tell her about the matching pajamas for people and their *cats*," Claudia snorted.

"Don't say that like you didn't buy a pair."

"I don't get it. So why are you always walking or using rideshare apps if you're loaded?" she asked.

"I got into a small car accident last year and since then I just don't like driving." Julianna shrugged and hit play on their movie.

Zuri looked at Gigi, curled up on her luxury dog bed next to the couch. Gigi looked back, the corners of her mouth turned slightly up, almost like she was smiling. Without her, she would never be sitting there on her couch with a good friend and even a girlfriend. She remembered talking to Paul, her neighbor down the street, when she'd first gotten Gigi and all their trips to the park. This was only the beginning. Gigi might not be enchanted to poop gold anymore, but she was definitely enriching Zuri's life in more ways than she would have thought possible. She was the real magic.

About the Author

B. E. Bang is a Denver-based science fiction and magical realism author.

She likes most dogs but loves Chow Chows, especially black ones.

When she isn't working or writing, Bang loves to spend time outdoors walking, running, biking and hiking. Bang also enjoys learning new languages and is currently brushing up on her Mandarin and beginning to learn Spanish.

Bang holds Master of Social Work and Master of Public Administration degrees from Arizona State University and a Bachelor of Arts in Asian Studies from the University of Denver.

Visit B. E. Bang online at www.bebangwrites.com.